THE NOOSE CLUB

David Bischoff

About the O. C. L. T. Series

There are incidents and emergencies in the world that defy logical explanation, events that could be defined as supernatural, extra-terrestrial, or simply otherworldly. Standard laws do not allow for such instances, nor are most officials or authorities trained to handle them. In recognition of these facts, one organization has been created that can. Assembled by a loose international coalition, their mission is to deal with these situations using diplomacy, guile, force, and strategy as necessary. They shield the rest of the world from their own actions, and clean up the messes left in their wake. They are our protection, our guide, our sword, and our voice, all rolled into one.

They are O.C.L.T.

Strong arms clutched his body. The fetid stench of dead flesh enveloped him. He gagged and tried to struggle, but felt helpless in the thing's grasp.

He was dragged toward the edge of the building, feet slipping and sliding on the rough surface of the roof.

"Remember your Dickens, old man? Remember Oliver Twist?" In another blur, the noose he'd been carrying since it was unearthed in the attic below was suddenly slipped over his head. "Well, Mr. Myth, give my regards to Bill Sykes."

And then, Bulfinch saw it.

Surrounded in a cape of squamous night, it flowed and drifted in bands of thorns and chains. Razor blades and Sweeny Todd swirled, shrieking, though the din. Snarling faces and images he could not bring into focus filled his vision.

With a huge lurching shove, Bullfinch was pushed toward the edge of the building.

The creature writhed. It writhed like a nest of snakes. It hissed and roared. Its sharp teeth gnashed. And it laughed.

Bullfinch was hurled backward. He was caught by the raised brick border just below the buttocks, but the force of the shove carried his head and torso over the edge and tilted him back over thin air.

Gasping, he tilted, reaching around and twisting down. The torque spun him around like an athlete doing a maneuver on a gymnastic horse. He clamped his legs, cried out, felt his grip slip… and he went over. With a surge of adrenalin and fear, he gripped the edge with his left hand, and held.

Mystique Press is an imprint of Crossroad Press.

Copyright © 2018 by David Bischoff
Cover by Dave Dodd
Design by Aaron Rosenberg
ISBN 978-1-946025-33-3

First edition

Tales of the O. C. L. T.

AVAILABLE NOW:

"Brought to Light—An O.C.L.T. Novella" by Aaron Rosenberg

"The Temple of Camazotz—An O.C.L.T. Novella" by David Niall Wilson

The Parting by David Niall Wilson

Incursion by Aaron Rosenberg

No Laughing Matter by Kurt Criscione

Lost Things by Melissa Scott & Jo Graham

Crockatiel! by David Niall Wilson

Disciples of the Serpent by Sidney Williams

Digging Deep by Aaron Rosenberg

UPCOMING:

Shades of Green by David Niall Wilson

Part One

All the infections that the sun sucks up
From bogs, fens, flats, on Prosper fall and make him
By inch-meal a disease! His spirits hear me
And yet I needs must curse. But they'll nor pinch,
Fright me with urchin—shows, pitch me i' the mire,
Nor lead me, like a firebrand, in the dark
Out of my way, unless he bid 'em; but
For every trifle are they set upon me;
Sometime like apes that mow and chatter at me
And after bite me, then like hedgehogs which
Lie tumbling in my barefoot way and mount
Their pricks at my footfall; sometime am I
All wound with adders who with cloven tongues
Do hiss me into madness.

—William Shakespeare
The Tempest, Scene II

Prologue

The noose.

It was a hangman's noose—an old one.

It had a history, that noose...

He fingered it. It felt smooth, and yet rough—like the skin of some ancient coiled snake.

He leaned over his desk and gazed at it.

As always, it seemed to stare back.

Jim Norse had discovered the thing in the attic of the house he'd purchased in the Whitaker neighborhood of Eugene, Oregon. It had lain at the bottom of a chest, tucked away deep in the shadows where it had been lost, or forgotten. The noose hadn't been the only thing in the chest. It had been filled with things his wife was excited to run past the antique shops — German and English knickknacks, and fine China.

But the noose had called to him, and before she could toss it out with the trash, he'd claimed it and secreted it away.

Gladys had gleefully gone through the antiques. They were not only of value—far more value than the usual glop you got in Oregon—but some of them were English. She was crazy about English things, and there'd been enough other pieces that she was able to justify keeping the ones she liked. All of the pieces she hadn't sold rested in various display cabinets throughout the house. She never stopped talking about them, but Jim had quit listening.

That noose though...

He knew exactly what it was, because he'd seen its like in a hundred old Western movies. It was a noose with a hangman's knot, a coil of rope shaped into a tube, designed to be loose enough to be placed around a victim's neck. When the victim dropped, whether from a horse with the rope tied around the branch of a tree, or more elaborately (and efficiently) from a high scaffold so the neck would break and death would be swifter, the tube would easily slide and allow the rope to tighten around the neck, cutting off the windpipe and suffocating the victim.

And it was old and frayed. It smelled of mothballs, and the hemp of the rope was of a different quality than used these days, rougher, not as cleanly woven.

He knew about its age and construction because he'd looked into it. He couldn't help himself.

He was fascinated with the damned thing.

I wonder, he thought often, *if this ever executed anyone.*

Some lynching perhaps. Lots of those back in the old days, when townsfolk and posses had taken the law into their own hands.

Jim Norse was a council member in the city of Eugene, Oregon. He hadn't always been so upstanding. He'd come to town in the '80s to see a Grateful Dead show and had stayed. He'd gotten married, started up a successful bike shop. When he'd expanded to a second shop and added a successful food cart business he'd found the time to get into local politics.

Even in Eugene, a paragon of liberal values, there were fights to be fought against the conservative right, the tea-bag Nazis, and their ilk. Nor was it hard to write letters, then editorials, then to canvass.

Soon, Norse had been working within the tie-dyed halls of Eugene government.

It had been a long time since he'd come to town and found the noose. Along the way, something even stranger had happened. At county fairs, in some of the local pubs, sometimes just walking down the street, he saw them. Others wore t-shirts with the logo of a noose silk-screened across the front. Others sported buttons; a few had bumper stickers. All of them sported some form of *The Noose.*

That was what he called it. Not "a noose," but "*The* Noose." He found such comfort in the bit of rope when his wife bitched at him, or his children acted up, that often he went up to the attic, sat at his special desk, smoked a joint, and then opened the large file drawer. He pulled the thing out, studied it, smelled it—sometimes he hugged it against his cheek (after a few tokes and maybe a big pull off a twenty-two-ounce bottle of Ninkasi Terminator Stout) and he felt better.

It wasn't just a noose, of course. It was attached to a long, thick rope, so there was no way he could carry it around with him. After a while, not wanting to be parted from it, he bought paper and pens and created a symbol—a special sketch of his noose, which he'd had printed up as patches to be embroidered on shirts and embossed on buttons. Like the others. It was his noose, but when he saw the others, he knew theirs were the same.

His wife complained. His kids thought he was weird, but then, one of the other buttons Jim Norse always wore read "Keep Eugene Weird," so they let it slide.

He saw the others everywhere. One was even a fellow member of the town council. When he approached them and showed them his buttons, or his patch, they did not seem surprised. Soon he stopped thinking in terms of them, and himself — he joined their number. "The Loose Noosers" they called themselves, because they had all found the same kind of nooses, and were fascinated by them. It should have seemed crazy—probably disturbing—but it didn't.

It wasn't like it was some kind of secret society. They just played poker, or went bowling, had a few beers here and there. His wife thought the others were fine, although she never liked his noose much. Out of respect, he never talked about it.

Things hadn't been going that well with Gladys lately, with or without the noose. Now that the kids were off to college, she was always on his case about this or that. To top it off, his seat at the council looked iffy for the next election. More and more he'd been taking comfort in the attic, listened to Phish or String Cheese Incident or yes, still the Dead (at that moment the Aug. 6, 1993, show at Autzen Stadium, Eugene, Oregon, was playing on his stereo) and contemplating his noose.

He gazed up to where he'd hung it from a rafter. Sometimes he put it up there so he could see it in action...waiting. Like a coiled beautiful snake. His favorite scene in any Western had always been the one where evil Henry Fonda had stuck the harmonica in young Charles Bronson's mouth while the boy's father balanced on top of his shoulders, a noose around his neck, in the ultimate spaghetti Western, *Once Upon a Time in the West*.

Now the noose seemed to call to him. He could almost hear the harmonica.

"Check it out," it seemed to say. "There's the chair. Go ahead. See how I feel around your neck."

1

Wendell "Mack" Macklemore **stared at the screen in front of** him. On either side of that screen, data streamed by, images and text, and on larger monitors hung above and beyond the three closest to him, more data passed through filters and search queries, seeking patterns and sluicing away the dreck.

The story that had caught his eye had appeared when a flag in one of his many search parameters flipped the right trigger three times within a geographic area. The page displayed was a news article from a newspaper in Portland, Oregon, and the image was that of a large old home, crime-scene tape crisscrossing the doors, and a bold headline reading "Third Death by Hanging in Two Months. Police Baffled."

He flipped quickly between the three stories, and then rolled his hand across his trackball and opened them on separate screens, side by side. All three deaths had happened within the city limits of Portland. All three were open cases without suspects, other than standard investigations into spouses and associates, all of whom had alibis. Two of three cases involved deaths that took place in the attic, and one in a basement. In all three cases, the door was locked from the inside. Police had to break into the two attics, and in the case of the basement death, a locksmith had been required to replace a key, the only copy being found in the victim's pocket.

Remarkably little evidence had been collected. All three victims were law-abiding citizens. All three were in committed relationships with no more than standard personal problems. On the surface, it looked more like the plot for a closed-room mystery novel than a real set of police reports.

The other thing was, Portland. There is a reason that a television series called *Portlandia* was created. The city edged into the fringe on many levels, and the addition of a strange series of murders hardly qualified to drive it into public recognition. There was no evidence of foul play. Even the fact that all of the deaths were by hanging, and all of the nooses used in those hangings were very similar and very old, had not really raised the kind of flags the same deaths might have in the heartland, or even in New York.

Mack hit keys mechanically, saving the files into a folder and almost simultaneously attaching them to emails. He addressed them to Reed Christopher Hayes and Geoffrey Bullfinch. Once he'd clicked SEND, without hesitation, he launched a new set of search algorithms, targeting activity involving nooses, locked rooms, and Portland, Oregon, looking for any sort of correlation.

He wasn't surprised that before he was finished the phone beside him buzzed. He picked it up without looking away from the screen.

"Mack," he said.

"I know who it is," Reed—better known as O.C.L.T. team leader R.C.—replied. "I called you—it's an internal extension."

Mack didn't reply, still scanning the data on the various screens.

"This thing in Portland," R.C. said. "You think it's more than local law enforcement can handle?"

"So far, they have exactly nothing. And they aren't asking for help, either, so logic indicates there will be more deaths with little response."

"Anyone in the area?"

"Not really, but I sent the files to Bullfinch. He's got a particular interest in the closed-room mysteries, and he has nothing pending. I am cross-referencing local investigators and police now, looking for a connection that will get us in the door."

"Keep me informed," R.C. said. "And Mack?"

"Yeah?"

"Any thoughts on what we might be up against?"

"Not so far. There seems to be no link to local folklore or legends. Considering the method of death, and the locked rooms, a spirit of some kind seems likely. Another reason for Bullfinch. If anyone knows how to track down local hauntings, it's him."

"Right, well, notify Isabella, and tell her to stay on call just in case. Bullfinch can take care of himself. Something tells me he's been doing so a lot longer even than he lets on, but it never hurts to be prepared."

"Old Boy Scout habits die hard," Max said. When R.C. didn't laugh, he added, "On it, of course. I'll keep the scans running, and I'll get a preliminary file out to Bullfinch."

"Do we have any kind of contact in the area?"

"There's an investigator there, a Madrigal Harper. She has a gifted, semi-autistic son named Skylar, and her love interest is a local police captain. Search just returned her. I'll send her information to Bullfinch. He'll be able to make official contact, and once that's done, if I can help I'll do so by the usual methods."

"Anonymous emails, helpful files…"

"Of course, and answers for any questions will be made available, through Bullfinch if possible, but by any means necessary if things get hairy."

"Keep me informed," R.C. said.

The phone went dead, and Mack, who always wore a headset, killed the line and returned his attention to the data on screen. He was tracking multiple threads, incidents in three other countries and four in the United States alone. It crossed the screen so quickly that it seemed impossible anyone could keep track, but Wendell Macklemore was far from an average hacker.

He ran security protocols and firewalls for half the countries in the free world, and many large businesses, while devoting the lion's share of his efforts to his work with the O.C.L.T. (Orphic Crisis Liaison Taskforce). It was his network—the web that connected governments, world leaders, and an unending flow of data, seeking anomalies—things beyond normal explanation that required special attention—and assigning that attention to taskforce members.

He considered ignoring the order to call in Isabella and hitting the road himself. Mack, along with his hacking skills, was an avid extreme sports enthusiast, and a visit to Portland could provide some interesting diversions, not to mention a shot at actually interfacing with an otherworldly entity. He and Bullfinch had worked together in the past—solving a bizarre spree of beheadings along the Mexican border. He'd also worked with another O.C.L.T. agent, Rebecca York, on a truly incredible adventure in Israel.

An alarm went off on the left-most screen, and he returned his focus to the moment. There would be other times and other cases. He studied the screen while, at the same time, typing an email to Isabella and sending it out through their secure server. He knew she'd just gotten back to the States after an extended trip to South America. A recent case in North Carolina had left her in the mood to hunt... and he was eager to hear what she'd found.

2

The face leered from the shadows. The moon was blood and the sea was alive with snakes. The stench was old horse piss.

She knew she had to find Sky before It found him.

"No, no, Madrigal. I'm coming for you."

The whole universe cackled and crowed.

"You okay, Mom?" asked Madrigal Harper's son Skylar. They were playing a board game with their friend Hildy. Maddy had been a thousand miles away.

"Yeah. You've been looking like me all day," said Hildy.

"Thanks," Maddy replied. "I couldn't sleep last night."

Nightmares. Horrible nightmares and premonitions.

Sky ignored them both, as was his habit.

"Hey, Mom, guess what?

"What?"

"I joined a cool new club at school."

"Oh?"

"Yep. It rocks. They like me! I think, anyway."

"Uh huh."

His words slipped in and out of her thoughts without really registering. What Maddy was focused on now was getting her mind off bad dreams and into strategy. Should she go for this… or go for that?

Madrigal "Maddy" Harper was an attractive, thirtyish brunette and a former parole officer turned private investigator. She lived in a big, well-kept trailer in Eugene, cheek to jowl with the ugliest Airstream ever to rust. That was Hildy's trailer. What she was used to was dreaming about chasing criminals and solving problems, not monsters and Armageddon.

"You have plenty of cards, kiddo," said Hildy. "Play them!"

Maddy squinted. "Yes. But I want to *win* this time."

"Look. It's not like we're playing some complicated extension. It's plain old plain old." Hildy got a weird look on her broad homely face, as though she was scratching at her memory. "And wait a minute, babe. Didn't you beat me and Bill last year?"

Maddy smiled at that. Especially at beating her boyfriend Bill in a game. He'd sulked for days.

"I did."

"And so?"

Maddy looked over at her teenage son, looking serene and angelic.

"I've never beaten *him*."

"So, Mom? Whatever. You will, you will. Some century. Listen to me, though. I just remembered this. And so the thing is, that we gotta stay up late sometimes for this club. They call it a society."

They were seated around a card table set up in the middle of Hildy's living room. Hildy's trailer was furnished in late twentieth-century Goodwill. An overstuffed sofa bed sat side by side with a tattered Barcalounger. Posters of Gloria Steinem and Joan Baez were pasted to the walls. Everything was arranged about a large entertainment center featuring a 1999 Sylvania TV set, a combo VCR/DVD player and cheap boom box. Huge stolid black RCA speakers stood to either side like the Indigo Girls frozen in concert. From all this spilled an ooze of video tapes and DVDs.

The place had that faintly sour thrift shop smell, combined with this week's batch of cool incense and a soupçon of cannabis. It was a scent that felt like home and comfy Mickey Mouse slippers.

"Late?" said Maddy. "If this involves girls...yes, yes, yes."

"Oh mom, get off it."

"Shut up, Maddy. The kid wants to say something important. So what's going on?" Hildy cut in.

"I guess what it is…" Sky looked sort of troubled now and subdued. "Well, it's a ghost hunting society."

"No shit. That's kind of awesome," said Hildy.

"What?" said Maddy.

The next words rushed out quickly. "Yes. It's called APP. Amalgamated Paranormal Police."

"That…that is a name," Hildy said, clapping him on the back.

What Maddy and her son and her best friend Hilda Bukowski were playing was the board game called The Settlers of Catan.

The Settlers of Catan was the first of the "nerd board games"—or "geek games." It had started in Germany, (board game freaks, those Germans) and spread. The guys on *The Big Bang Theory* played it, but it was really simple enough even for their dumb-blonde neighbor Penny.

Anyway, it was *also* simple enough for Maddy to play.

"Okay. I'm going to use these cards here," she said, giving the cards back to the 'Bank,' "and buy myself a road."

"Cool," said Hildy. "Cool."

"Oh. I see," said Maddy, frowning. "You say cool, because your mission in this game is to screw me over!"

That's what Maddy thought, even though there was that "thief" she was guilty of planting as close to Hildy as she could when she got control. All's fair…

"Did Bill say he was coming by tonight?" asked Hildy.

"Yep. But he's just stopping by to say hi and isn't going to stick around. Lots of extra work to clear up downtown." Maddy shook her head. "If the taxpayers knew how hard policemen have to work on limited funds these days…"

"You mean the 'pigs'?" asked Skylar.

He seemed all innocent about the term.

That was the thing about Sky. Maddy knew he was a low-level autistic (used to be called Asperger's Syndrome) but still it shocked her sometimes the stuff he came out with.

"Yeah," said Sky. "Off the pigs! Right on!"

"Inappropriate, Sky," she said. "'Pigs' is a negative term for police officers created by protesters at rallies in the nineteen-sixties."

"Oh. Back when you were in college, right, Mom?"

Hildy laughed. "Yep. Getting tear-gassed."

Maddy glared at Hildy. "Skylar. Your mother graduated from Oregon State University in nineteen ninety-three. She's not *that* old. During the Democratic convention of nineteen sixty-eight—a famous confrontation between rebellious youth of the time—she was very, very young."

"Yep. The kid can do math. Don't get too literal," Hildy chuckled.

Maddy was still only half paying attention.

"Excellent," said Skylar. "I shall have to research that."

"Just don't call Bill a pig," she said.

"No. That's your mom's job when she's mad at him." Hildy said.

She could have really gone off on Hildy then, but that actually got a smile out of Skylar. Sky got a joke! Hope once more bloomed in her breast.

Skylar didn't get jokes that often. He didn't make jokes, with a few rare and feeble exceptions. Every day of her life she thanked Providence that he wasn't highly autistic. He had friends and enjoyed speaking with people, but he simply didn't experience the full range of human emotion.

He had his passions, but they often seemed more like obsessions. He was into cards and comic books, which he collected. He enjoyed stamps and coins, which he also collected. He didn't read regular fiction, but he liked sci-fi TV shows and movies. He didn't need to collect those, they were bloody everywhere these days.

Maddy sighed.

It was now, it seemed, a low-level autistic world.

The full range of human emotions.

Hmm.

Maybe Sky was the lucky one. He would have to deal on an emotional level with people like Bill.

"Bill tells me mom's always yelling at him," said Skylar.

"Only when he deserves it!" she said, feeling self-righteous.

"Okay, okay," said Hildy. "Enough with *True Romance*. Let's back to some serious Settling!"

Maddy was a Victory Point shy of winning (by her calculations) when Bill showed up. There was a knock at the door, then the police captain entered the room, gave her a brief smack on the lips, and settled down in the spare seat at the table.

"Gee, Maddy, "Bill said. "You look tired. There are bags under the bags under your eyes."

"Fuck you. I told you I couldn't sleep last night," she retorted.

"Hey you," Bill said to Sky.

Sky looked up, nodded and returned his focus to the game.

"Howdy, Bully," Bill said, turning to Hildy and allowing a mild Texas twang into his voice.

"Howdy, Baldy," she answered. "You hungry? I've got some old meatloaf and bean salad somewhere in the back of the fridge."

"Hmmm. Tempting as roadkill fresh off of a Springfield mill road, but I'll pass. I could use a cold one though. Gotta get back to work."

Maddy laid down her cards, rose, and went to the fridge. She pulled out a Pabst Blue Ribbon. PBR. You had great beer up here in the Pacific Northwest now and what did he always want? PBR. Well, he was a cheap date, anyway.

"Drinking on duty, Baldy?" Hildy teased.

"PBR ain't drinking, Bully. And as I'm on my own time, I can do what I want."

"What are you doing?"

"Sorry. Right now that's way classified. Let's just say, damned important stuff." He chortled and rolled his eyes. "Oh man! This game. You beat the hell out me in this one, Junior."

Sky seemed smug about that. "I did, didn't I?"

"Wish I could stay to have another go. But remember—we have to play poker sometime. Your ass is mine, kid. Just bring those pennies."

"I am currently studying the game," Sky said, trying not to smile.

He focused.

Maddy handed Bill his beer. He took a drink but suddenly seemed remote. His eyes kind of glassed over, like he was thinking about something. Maddy knew the look. He was full of small talk, but his mind was miles away. It had to be another big case at headquarters.

She tried to ignore him, but his expression put her off her game. She didn't know what was getting to him, but she wanted to pull him out of it. She wanted some more of his attention. She got precious little of it as it was.

"So guess what," she said. "Sky has joined a ghost hunting group. And there are girls in it!"

Bill looked up. "What? What did you say, Maddy?" He was a handsome brute with a low brow and a big chin, but with eyes that twinkled like emeralds sometimes. He had big, strong shoulders and sometimes when she looked at him, Maddy still got a little weak in her knees.

"I said, there are girls in it."

"No. The first part."

"Sky has joined a Ghost Hunting Group."

"That true, Sky King?"

"Yes! It looks to be a remarkable adventure."

She thought he was going to say something like, *Son, girls are the adventure.*

Instead, he said, "Hmm. Well…Hmm."

He watched the rest of the game thoughtfully, sipping at his beer.

When they were finished, so was his beer.

And somehow, despite Maddy's concentration, Sky had won again.

Well, at least Hildy didn't win, she thought, amused.

"So, Skylar. Congrats. I think we've got a rematch comin' up, right?" Bill said.

"Excellent!"

"As long as these other fine players will join us."

"Sounds good to me," said Maddy.

"Now though, about this ghost hunter's club. At your school?"

"Yes. It's informal. Just a bunch of us got interested, is all."

"You don't seem to be…uhm…the kind?"

"Oh, but I'm the skeptic of the group! It's just for fun. But I must say, wouldn't it be a scientific breakthrough to discover the real cause of ghostly manifestations and other psychic phenomena?"

"That it would, son. Say—if we at the Eugene Police have a ghost problem—we could consult with you?"

"I would need supervision from my mother. I'm sure that would induce a fee."

He looked at his mother.

It was her turn to smile.

3

He stood up on the chair.

He fitted the noose around his neck.

It felt so good. Like a sweet lover's caress.

Don't you feel better now? said the voice from nowhere. *Don't you feel like you are under control? Don't you remember that you can take the noose off or leave it on—and you are close to your departed loved ones?*

"Yes," said the man. "Yes."

Good, said the voice, suddenly assuming an edge like the Demon Barber's razor. *Because you're wrong!*

A sudden force struck both the man and his chair.

The force was stronger than his balance; the chair was just a rickety antique. It was knocked free and flung several feet away.

He dropped like a stone.

Only a short distance.

The noose tightened like a tourniquet and he started to swing, kicking and spasming, caught in a slow-motion strangle.

"Sir?"

Bill turned to the dispatcher and hesitated.

"There's a man waiting in your office," she said.

Bill frowned.

"I'm not expecting anyone. Who is it?"

"I've never seen him before, sir. I told him you weren't here, but he asked to wait. I hope you don't mind my letting him into your office…"

He did, actually, but he decided to let it pass. He was tired, and the sooner he got in, found out who was looking for him, and got them back out, the sooner he could return to work. He smiled thinly.

"Thank you," he said. "I'll sort it out."

He headed down the hall, trying not to let his face twist into a scowl. The last thing he needed was some new crackpot wasting his time. Portland was full of every sort of oddball the world had to offer, and far too often they found their way to his office with their theories, complaints, strange ideas, and stranger stories. Normally, he took that as part of the job, but with bodies piling up, and any real progress eluding him, his patience had worn thin.

As he entered his office, a tall, slender man rose from where he was seated by the door. The stranger had hair gone gray, a neatly trimmed beard, and held a worn fedora in one hand. He wore khakis, a plain white shirt, no tie, and a pair of worn boots that looked to have traveled more than a few miles. The hand without the hat in it extended, and almost without thought, Bill held out his own and shook it.

"Captain Bill Edmonds?" the man said. His accent was strange, hinting of European heritage, but oddly generic and a little formal.

"Guilty," Bill said. "And you are?"

"Bullfinch," the man replied. "Geoffrey Bullfinch. I've come a very long way to see you—I hope it's not a bad time."

Bill remembered his scowl, but for some reason it seemed inappropriate.

"It's never a good time around here," he said. "What can I do for you, Mr. Bullfinch?"

"I'm hoping you have that question backward," Bullfinch said. "I've come to offer my assistance."

Bill studied the man, found nothing crazy or ambiguous, and replied. "With? If you are looking for a consulting position, I'm afraid we have no current funding for anything like that."

"I'm more of a subject matter expert," Bullfinch said. "I understand that you have a rash of very strange deaths here—suicides, according to news reports, but I have my doubts."

The scowl finally found Bill's face.

"Have a seat, Mr. Bullfinch," he said. "I'm going to give you a couple of minutes of my time because, frankly, all of the ways I've spent it on this case so far have resulted in wasting it. We have released very little information to the press, or the public... I'm a bit surprised to see it register on anyone's radar so quickly."

"The organization that I represent is uniquely locked into a variety of sources," Bullfinch said. "The number of similar cases and the small geographic footprint set off triggers. As I understand it, each of these 'suicides' took place behind a locked door. No way in, and yet, at this point there have to be questions of murder..."

Bill stared for a moment, trying to decide if he should trust this man, have him tossed out on his ear, or arrest him for questioning. So far, nothing Bullfinch had said was information not readily available, but it was the way he unhesitatingly tied it all together that set off alarms.

"There has been nothing to indicate that any of the victims had a reason to be particularly suicidal. There is no connection between the victims, except... on two of the three, we found items—a card and a pinback button—with a picture of a noose very similar to the ones they were hanging from when we found them."

"I understand they are old," Bullfinch said. "The nooses, I mean, antiques? And very similar?"

This was not information that was readily available.

"How would you know that?" he said.

"Just accept, for the moment, that I do," Bullfinch said. "Surely the similarity indicates a connection?"

Bill sat back, and this time the frown came easily.

"Of course," he snapped, immediately regretting the outburst. "There has to be a connection. The nooses in question—you understand this is not to be spread to the public, particularly the media?"

Bullfinch nodded. "Of course."

"They aren't just similar. They are identical. The rope is very old, and we've had each authenticated for age… but damned if it's not like the same bit of rope is being used, over and over again, to kill people, and by someone clever enough to do so and not only leave no clues, but also to set the scene so that suicide is going to be very difficult to disprove. Without that, I may not even be able to get the city's support to keep the investigation open."

"I imagine that if enough locals hang themselves, even the stodgiest of bureaucrats will have to get on board," Bullfinch said.

"I'm not inclined to let more people die to justify the investigation," Bill said. "Hell, too many have died already." In any case, none of this tells me why you are here."

"The organization I work for, privately funded, I assure you, has an interest in cases and situations where the circumstances appear—how should I put it? —out of the ordinary. My own expertise is in folklore, legends, and what basis they have had over the years in fact. It's inevitable that someone, eventually, is going to try and work your city into a frenzy over these killings with stories of ghosts or something supernatural. It's human nature."

"Ghosts are not hanging people in Portland, Oregon, Mr. Bullfinch," Bill said. "Someone very real, very alive, and very evil is doing that. It's my job to find out who that person is, and to put them away for a very long time. I'm afraid I don't have any time for nonsense."

"Quite right," Bullfinch said smoothly. "I, on the other hand, have all the time in the world for it, the knowledge and expertise to combat foolishness, should it arise, and what I hope are some actually significant insights into similar cases. In most of those cases, things turned out exactly as you say—a man, or a woman, giving the impression of being something more."

"Most?" Bill said.

Bullfinch just smiled.

Bill shook his head, reached up and rubbed his temple, and managed a smile of his own.

"Do you drink, Mr. Bullfinch?"

"I've been known to imbibe on occasion."

Bill stood, walked to the door of his office, and flipped the lock. He returned to his desk, unlocked the file drawer on the left side of his desk, and pulled out two tumblers and a bottle labeled "Billy Whiskey". Bullfinch raised an eyebrow and watched as Bill poured two fingers into each tumbler and slid one across the desk.

"It's local," he said. "Aged two years in oak barrels, and made using a very old cognac still brought over from France. One thing about Portland, there are a lot of crackpots, but in between you find the artisans."

"Bourbon?" Bullfinch said.

"Of a sort. If you are a whiskey drinker, you'll taste a hint of molasses and maybe a drop of hazelnut in the mix. They only make it in small batches."

"I didn't place you as a connoisseur of fine spirits," Bullfinch said, lifting his glass and taking a quick whiff of the aroma.

"I'm more of a beer guy," Bill said. "I love this stuff, but I'll tell you...I only bought it because it says 'Billy' on the label."

The two men drank in silence. Then, as if just remembering, Bullfinch raised an eyebrow.

"I meant to ask you," he said. "There is a local investigator I am hoping to make contact with. Perhaps you know her? Her name is Madrigal Harper."

He hangs for a moment, the man.

Just hangs, spinning softly as though pushed by some phantom breeze. His face has turned purple. His eyes are bugged open, as though something from behind is trying to push the eyeballs out. A thread of spittle hangs from the lips, suspended like a tear of mucous, and then drops to the floor of the attic.

And then, suddenly, the feet, shoes already kicked off, spasm once, twice, three times. The body shudders, twists.

Stiffens.

Grows limp.

From a dark corner, a chuckle emerges and fills the room like some foul-smelling gas, ancient as evil.

4

Attached to Eugene, Oregon, at about buttocks level, squats sister city, Springfield.

There are many Springfields in the United States of America. All Springfields believe they were the inspiration for *The Simpsons*, that iconic, immature American Springfield, with a nuclear power plant, Moe's Tavern, and of course, "Doh!"

Springfield, Oregon's main advantage in this amazing cultural race is that Matt Groening was from Oregon, had of course been to Springfield many times in the days of its great stinky sawmills and factories, and knew it for the working-class heart of the U.S. that it was.

The afternoon after he met Captain Edmonds, Bullfinch got into the Chevrolet Spark he'd rented at the Mahlon Sweet Airport and drove from the scenic campus of the University of Oregon to a strip bar in Springfield.

The drive was beautiful. It was a gorgeous autumn day with puffy cumulus clouds playing slow-motion bumper cars in an azure sky. The air smelled fresh and clean, bathed in what had been a cool and breezy night. Just past the campus and the new Matthew Knight Arena, a small butte grew from the ground like a forest giant's mole, sprouting trees and houses, serene above the buzz and whirl of I-5. To his right swung the majestic Willamette River, plunging through Eugene like a blue-green artery. And then, hiding the river, was a series of pawnshops, U-Haul™ offices, and gas stations, which was Glenwood, a kind of no man's land between Springfield and its kin.

He came to a bridge where a WELCOME TO SPRINGFIELD

sign stuck out and then dropped into pure, low-rent Americana.

Bullfinch checked his GPS. He loved this new-fangled technology. Email, cell phones, electronic cars. He'd listened to Mack going on for hours about it, but wasn't sure the boy truly understood the magic. Bullfinch had lived for a very, very long time, and he had perspective most men lacked.

A Mendelssohn etude played on KWAX, the local classical station as he tooled up Main Street, Springfield.

The town looked as though once upon it had been bombed out and patched up.

Chinese Restaurant. Taco Bell. A bar. Another bar. Yet another bar. And, oh look, another bar.

Down the road a bit was an adult store ("Sex is its own reward, but only if you do it right") in crooked letters on a sign near the latest porno DVD sale, then a discount grocery store, coin laundry, and pawn shop. Pizza place. Biker bar. Auto parts vendor.

Across the road was a tractor sales store with a big sign—I INHALED FREQUENTLY. THAT WAS THE POINT.

And then, finally, after a long curve, there it was.

JIGGLES.

Bullfinch turned into the ample parking lot. It was a big place and a lot of the Oregon road bars looked like fifties or sixties architecture, one story. Nice. Plenty of expensive cars and trucks (including one of those trucks with wheels taller than the car he was driving) in the parking lot. Beside the door was a sign that gave the bar's name, along with a Las Vegas-style neon design depicting a partially clad woman.

Bullfinch parked, climbed out of the Spark, and stared at the place. Not his type of establishment, though, as with almost everything new, it intrigued him. He would have preferred a café, or a neighborhood bar, but this one wasn't his call.

He crossed the parking lot and took stock of his surroundings. The entrance was in the lower rear. Bullfinch opened the door. NO DAMNED DRUGS! read the next sign. He was immediately struck by a blast of loud rap music and a glimpse of shimmering naked flesh.

He stepped back into the sunlight, fumbled in the pockets of his tweed jacket and pulled out a case. From the case he withdrew two earplugs. Once inserted, he braved the entrance once more.

After the brightness of the sun, the darkened interior of the club was difficult to navigate. He wandered in slowly. To the left side was a DJ booth, to the right the stage. His eyes slowly adjusted to the dim light, and the blare of the rap music crashing around him was dulled somewhat by the earplugs.

On the stage in front of him, a bit of a pit created by walls, was a golden pole. A lithe dancer twirled around it like something from an R-rated Cirque du Soleil. She had dark, flowing hair and plenty of curves. Bullfinch turned away and scanned the club as his eyes adjusted to the dim light.

There was just one man at the front sitting behind a wrinkled dollar bill. A number of tables were lined up behind him, but only a couple of other customers sat around them. Most of the club's patrons were at the taller tables in the back, or playing at slot machines by the bar. They seemed engrossed in conversations with another group of women who circled and hovered there. Obviously strippers as well, they wore bikinis or skimpy outfits. One young woman seemed to have forgotten to put her top back on.

Sitting at the far end of those tables was the man he was there to meet. He went to the table and lifted his hat. "Philip?"

As though he saw Bullfinch every day, the man turned his moon face. "Well, well, well. The minor comes to pay homage to the major—at last! Take a load off, Hamilton."

Bullfinch, of course, was annoyed. One of Philip Roman's favorite things to do when they spoke was to call him "Edith" or "Hamilton".

"You mock my family name, sir!" he said in a comic huff. "Duel at dawn! Mystery trivia."

"I don't get up at dawn or anytime for a long time thereafter," said Phil Roman, chuckling. "Happy to take up the gauntlet some evening though. Now sit, sit! My beer is running out. Buy yourself a drink and me one as well."

As though on cue, a waitress appeared. "What'll you have, Mr.?" She was pretty. Chewing gum.

"Whatever beer this man is drinking...and another for him."

He took out his wallet and removed a twenty-dollar bill.

"Dead Guy Ale!" said Phil. "My favorite from Rogue Brewery. One of the first and best of the Oregon microbreweries."

"Ah. Excellent." Bullfinch scuffed the chair back and sat, offering his hand. "Good to finally see you again."

Roman stared at the hand as though it were something foul. "I don't shake hands."

"Ah. I forgot. Sorry."

"But damned good to see you too, fella!" Roman's face peeled back in a grin. He had a bowl cut of dark hair with a bit of a monk's tonsure baldness in the back. Dyed black, clearly. A beard of faintly grayer hair strapped this on uncertainly. The bulges in the man's chin made it look like the whole business might fall off at any minute.

Roman was about six feet tall. He wore tan workpants and a huge jean jacket over a black t-shirt with holes in it, displaying the image of that gorgeous female model of the '50s, Bettie Page.

It was odd, but despite the music's volume, Bullfinch had no trouble hearing his companion. And Roman seemed to be able to hear him. He would have far preferred to meet the fellow in some convivial pub or coffee bar for their chat, but he was familiar enough with the man's personality to know that you had to do things his way or not at all.

"I'm glad you agreed to meet me, Phil."

"You mean you didn't come to Eugene just to see me?"

"It's an opportunity."

"You must see my new acquisitions. And there's always that first edition of M.L. James you've wanted. We could haggle a bit, hmm? A steak at Psycho Steak House— ha ha, pardon me—Bates

Steak House would go a long way to lowering my price."

"I would like nothing more," Bullfinch said. "I'm not on a pleasure trip, though, so I believe that this time I'll have to pass. I'm doing some research, and I wanted to look at purchasing anything you have, non-fiction-wise, about local ghosts.

Philip Roman was a book dealer. One of the best in America. He specialized in mystery, but he had a fine selection of counter-culture material and the outré, including books about the supernatural, folklore, legends...and ghosts.

"Local ghosts," said Roman, raising fine, long eyebrows. "Local ghosts? As in Eugene and Springfield? I ask because, of course, Portland up north specializes in those!"

"Oh, of course. Mythology, like your ancestors. Whatever, really." He took a long pull on his beer.

Bullfinch also took a large sip of the Dead Guy Ale. It wasn't bad. A bit too hoppy for his taste. But...wait...nice aftertaste. Yes. Good!

Bullfinch loved beer and it was refreshing to have these American microbreweries to sample. Brewing was an ancient art, and one he had followed with some interest. Some of the newer iterations were very intriguing.

He sipped again.

"So," said Roman. "Ghosts. Books. Well, I think I might have a few...for sale. I'm not a lending library you know. I'm a bookseller."

"Oh no, Phil. I have adequate funds."

"Good. Just so you understand. It's not every day I invite people to actually view my books in their natural habitat. My home."

"I understand... I wouldn't presume..."

A strong, assertive voice interrupted him.

"Philip Roman. I have a gun in my jacket pocket, loaded with a bullet with your name on it. Do you want it in your head here or outside?"

Bullfinch turned, startled.

The idea of a man wanting to kill Phil Roman was not one that he thought improbable. And a strip bar, no matter how friendly, was still a strip bar. He'd been in rougher places, and he readied himself for whatever was coming next.

The man he faced when he turned, however, was no Al Capone. It was a tall man with a friendly grin.

"Hey! You must be Mr. Bullfinch. Welcome to Oregon!"

Bullfinch found a bare hand thrust his way. He shook the hand. It was a good, hearty, American handshake.

Behind the hand was a good-looking fellow in his late thirties with a touch of gray to his sideburns and a smile as big as the great Oregon outdoors. He wore a simple Polo shirt and shorts, overtopped with a University of Oregon zippered green sweatshirt. Still he looked and sounded more East Coast than West.

"I am Geoffrey Bullfinch."

"Well, it's a real pleasure to meet you. I read your great-great-grandfather's book in college. Wonderful. Important man. Glad you're carrying on his work."

"Okay, okay, cut the bull, Ralph. Sit down, will you?"

"Sure, Phil. Got your book."

Phil grunted but couldn't help smiling.

"The Hardman? From nineteen seventy-seven? And signed?"

"Yep."

The smile got bigger. "And I didn't believe you. What are your sources?"

"Ah, but that would be telling, wouldn't it big guy?" Ralph clapped Phil on the shoulder, sat down. He pulled out a paperback book in a Mylar plastic encasement and gave it to Phil.

"I'll look at it later." He in turn pulled out an envelope. "I hope this works."

Ralph's face brightened ever further. He took the envelope casually and tucked it away in his pocket. "Lynn says hi, by the way."

"You ought to bring her along sometime to this place. I see plenty of women enjoying the dancing here."

"Oh, no. Not Lynn. She doesn't approve. Take it from me." Ralph turned. "I'm really sorry, Mr. Bullfinch. The name's Ralph White. Buddy of Phil's. Fairly new, but time isn't important, is it?"

"Now there I can agree with Phil, Ralph," said Bullfinch. "I myself am feeling younger with every moment I spend in your remarkable state."

"Yep. Great place. But hey—you lookin' into the Bigfoot myth? Phil wouldn't say."

"Ralph. He's looking for spooks."

"Ghosts?"

"Well, in a word… Yes. I suppose that's quite true."

"Hmmm. You're English, aren't you? Plenty of ghosts back there, or so I've been told. Haven't heard of too many here in Oregon."

"It is a young state, even in respect to most American history, Ralph. However… well… I'm really not at liberty. I've done business with Philip Roman here for many, many years, and I have to say, there is no finer mystery and occult bookman in your country. And in Oregon. You'd think one of the fellows in New England would have a better selection. Thanks to the Internet, not so anymore and Phil here is a master of finding remarkable things."

Phil held up his paperback in its Mylar sleeve and laughed heartily.

"Hmm. Well, I help him a bit," said Ralph.

"Ralph's more of a modern mystery buff," said Phil. "Of course, there are a lot of people who help… that's how it all works."

"Hey. I like the pulps too. And fifties and sixties original paperbacks!"

"I suppose. In any case, he's a businessman and so is his wife, Lynn."

Ralph White beamed. "You bet. Right now we run the Mama's Original Italian. You must come over and have a meal!"

"I'd be happy to," said Bullfinch.

Ralph whipped out a card and gave it Bullfinch. "Couldn't have done it without my buddy Phil here."

"Lynn got my Chicago ready yet?" asked Phil.

"Working on it, Phil. Working on it."

"You come here often?" said Bullfinch.

"Nope. Only when Phil wants to meet. Always here."

"I see."

"Hey! Mr. Bullfinch. It's just hitting me."

"Oh."

"Yeah." Ralph scratched his head. "You say you're interested in Eugene ghosts? As a matter of fact, just this year they've started doing 'Ghost Tours'."

"Ghost tours?"

"Yeah. Matter of fact, it's Friday? Right?"

"All day," Phil said.

Ralph White laughed. "Cool. Maybe you should go. Ghosts can't hurt you. And Eugene ghosts probably wear tie dye, but if anyone knows who you should talk to, or who knows about ghosts, they're probably part of that tour."

"Oh?" said Bullfinch.

"Sure, in Eugene, Oregon, where hippies go to die, they become…the Grateful Dead!"

5

Flies buzzed around the hanging body.

Bill still held the handkerchief over his mouth and nose, so the stench wasn't as overpowering, but it was bad.

How could a body decompose so quickly?

The guy was naked. Below him was a pile of feces and urine. He'd evacuated himself upon death. But more than that, he'd been eviscerated as well, and his intestines hung down all the way to the floor, a waterfall of tripe. His face was an over-ripe purple. Maggots squirmed in his rotting eyeballs.

Edmonds took this all in. Snapshot.

"Okay, I got it," he said. "Cut him down and get the medical examiner and the CSIs in here."

He hurried back down to the hall and leaned against an open window, taking in some fresh fall air to help stifle the urge to heave. He turned to an officer standing nearby.

"So, sergeant, let me get this straight," he said. "Wife comes home this afternoon. Attic door is locked. From inside?"

"Yes, sir."

"And you've checked all the windows?"

"Yes, sir. Locked fast. Not even any prints—they're coated with dust."

"So, you're telling me, basically, that this guy hangs himself, and then cuts himself open." It wasn't a question.

"I think it has to be the other way around, sir. Has to be."

"Good point. I guess he could have cut himself open while standing on the chair, and then hanged himself...but it still doesn't play. What we have here isn't just another mysterious hanging. It's another locked-room mystery. Number fuckin' four!"

6

"Wow, Mom. Cool. Did you hear that?"

Maddy Harper turned to Skylar. There was that weird glint in his eyes. She caught the whiff of his new obsession. Ghosts.

Around them was the din and clatter of nighttime Eugene on a Friday night. Once upon a time, when the malls had moved into the suburbs and suddenly the city started charging for parking downtown, Eugene had died. Now, though, it had somehow risen from the grave. There were nightclubs, movie houses, and bars. Pizzerias and restaurants. The downtown holes had been filled in (there had been a huge one in front of the library where some idiots had pulled out the old Sears building and then stopped work) and suddenly now, there was life. And doughnut shops! In fact, this whole "Ghost Tour" had started in front of the infamous Voodoo Donuts, a 24-hour joint spawned out of Portland. Before they'd begun, they'd been treated to a short lecture on voodoo.

They were a pretty large group, just on their own, with Skylar, Maddy, Hildy, Bill, and Geoffrey Bullfinch. Bill had made the introductions, a little surprised to see Bullfinch again so soon.

"This should be right up your alley," he'd said, once they were all on a first-name basis. He was out of uniform and a lot more relaxed than when the two had first met.

They stood in front of city Hall with a half-dozen other locals and tourists. This was the place where there was drumming on Saturdays during the famous Saturday Market. Drumming circles to be exact. Bill was never sure what to think of Eugene. One minute it seemed quaint and historic, and the next he felt like he was living in the middle of a huge can of mixed nuts.

"Now my assistant is going to pass out the dowsing rods I promised," said the attractive young tour guide. "You can use these to contact any spirits floating about here. Perhaps even the poor hanged man."

The assistant, obviously a college student, handed out what appeared to be coat hangers, bent, with cardboard handles.

"Are these coat hangers?" asked Hildy.

"No. They need to be copper rods to function properly." Bullfinch observed. "It's a matter of conductivity."

Maddy turned and glanced at him. He was an older gentleman, dressed a little oddly. He smiled, and took the *dowsing rod* that was offered to him.

She thought he looked kind of natty in that fedora and tweed coat. *If I was a little older...* she thought.

"Okay," their guide continued, "the idea is to ask questions and try to make contact. Your dowsing rods are where you will feel the connection, if there is one. No activity is no. But if the wires cross—the answer is yes."

"Wouldn't no activity mean nothing is happening too?" Bill asked.

The guide ignored him.

"Mom. Mom. Who are you going to talk to?" Sky asked.

"I've always wondered if the spirit of Jerry Garcia is anywheres about?" she said. "I mean, we were his country cousins, and his grandchildren sure pound those drums every weekend. Jerry Garcia?" She turned her eyes up to the sky. "Are you here?"

The rods did not move.

"Cool. I'm going to ask that hanged guy if he's here."

"No no, please," said Bullfinch. "Let me."

"Sure! Awesome. Bill says you're the ghost guy! I knew you were coming to town, but I didn't know you'd be here."

"I didn't know 'here' existed until earlier this week," Bullfinch said. "Couldn't miss a chance for some local research."

Maddy turned to her son and cocked her head, but didn't ask. She'd been there for Bill's introduction, and there had been no real mention of Bullfinch being a "ghost guy". A question for a later time.

"Dan Finch," said Bullfinch. "Are you with us?"

The wires crossed immediately.

Skylar's jaw dropped. "Wow!"

"Did you just do that?" Hildy asked. She stared down at the wires in her hands and shook them.

"I did not," Bullfinch said. "Very interesting. Shall I ask him more questions then?"

"Yeah!" said Skylar.

Bullfinch moved the wires back into neutral positions.

"Dan Finch. Were you hanged in this place?"

The wires crossed immediately. *Yes.*

"Holy crap!" said Hildy. "I think I'm getting the hell out of here."

She'd come along at Maddy's request, not out of any particular personal desire to mingle with ghosts. In fact, she'd bought a baker's dozen donuts and was now shaking hands with a bear claw.

The guide laughed. "Oh, don't worry. That happens all the time. He is here, no question."

Maddy looked over to Bullfinch. Bullfinch coughed and shrugged again.

"Shit!" said Bill Edmonds. "What the hell. I'll ask him a question. But in my mind, right?"

"Well, he's listening for sure now!"

Edmonds closed his eyes.

For a moment, the traffic cacophony grew still. An autumnal silence seemed to hover. Above them scooted galleons of clouds in a sea of night. The moon had risen early, almost full, and seemed somehow close to them, like a big pockmarked eye, peering.

Again, despite herself, Maddy shivered.

Bill stared down at the rods. His lips moved, but he said nothing.

Pause. Nothing.

And then, slowly but certainly, the rods moved together.

Yes, the spirit was saying.

"Jesus!" said Edmonds.

As though bitten by a snake, he let go of the rods. They clattered to the cement.

The guide said, "Sir! What happened?"

"It was like some kind of electrical shock."

"You okay?"

He was rubbing his hands. "Yeah, yeah, I'm fine."

"I'm so sorry. That's never happened before."

"Look. Don't worry about it. I'm fine. Don't make a big deal of it. It's all bullshit anyway."

The guide frowned, but didn't argue.

Maddy shot a glance at Bullfinch.

Bullfinch was frowning.

Maddy noticed then that Geoffrey Bullfinch had *also* dropped his dowsing rods.

7

His name was Adam Even.

Adam Horowitz was his given name, but he'd started in the comedy business as Adam Hadem, and had made a slight splash on the Borsht Belt. He'd earned enough to head from New York to Hollywood.

That was back in the Seventies. Comedy had been pretty. Adam did well, and looked good on screen. He'd scored a minor, non-speaking part as one of the frat fools in *National Lampoon's Animal House*. He'd hung out with John Belushi and Curtis Salgado at Taylor's near the University of Oregon campus, listening to Robert Cray.

One night, Belushi, drunk and stoned, had turned and said to him, "You know. I gotta talk to Danny about this Blues stuff. I got an idea."

Animal House was a surprise hit.

Adam got more work in L.A. Bit parts, yeah. But then he got involved with the improv scene. Riding on the success of artists like Robin Williams, that scene exploded. Adam could do it. He got gigs.

He knew the score. Some nights you killed. That wasn't hard, especially with a snoot full of coke. Man, some nights you died. And you went out then maybe you did something harder than coke.

But Steve Martin was right, Adam had mused later on, sitting and rotting in his house out beside River Road in Eugene. What you had to learn wasn't to kill every night. It was to be good every night.

Comedy is hard. Dying is easy.

And then, along came *Animal House 2*. Bluto's Little Jewish Buddy.

As it happened, Adam was watching Robin Williams in *Mrs. Doubtfire* when a knock had brought him to the door. It was the middle of the afternoon and he was expecting a package of old books he'd bought on eBay.

Instead of the postman, though, it was Phil Roman.

"He's still alive!" said Phil. "He's still alive! How have you been?"

"What's up, Phil?"

"Whatcha watching?" said Phil.

"*Mrs. Doubtfire*. Robin Williams."

"I just got two free weeks on Netflix. I'm getting three films every day. I wanna see this one on your TV!"

Adam said, "Phil. You might have called first."

"I'm just a few houses away."

"True."

"So here it is." Phil thrust the envelope out proudly. "*House of Wax*. 3D."

"No shit."

"No. I got it because…"

"Because you know I got a TV capable of 3D and Blu-ray and pretty damned much anything."

"Yep."

"And you needed somewhere to watch it…"

"Right again."

Adam wanted to kick the asshole out. He wanted to be alone. But Phil was a smart guy.

The Shadow knows…

"Vincent Price, right?"

"Yep."

"And Charles Bronson!"

"That's it."

Adam Even pushed the door open wide enough to accommodate Phil's girth.

"Okay."

"Got some popcorn?"

"Sure."

"Not that generic crap, I hope."

"Uhm. No, Phil. Grade A Movie Theater."

Phil waddled toward the living room, where he knew Adam kept his 60-inch 3D-enabled LG giant screen. Phil's own TV was an old Sylvania tube number that still worked. He could have afforded one of the big new ones, but didn't want to spend that kind of money. Not when others would spend it for him.

Phil eased his hefty frame down onto a couch. "Didn't sit in your chair that time."

"You just didn't want to have to get up again right away when I kicked you out."

"Hey, hey. True, true."

Phil picked up a copy of the day's *Register Guard*, the local newspaper, and started reading. "You mentioned popcorn."

"Yeah. Just a minute. Ice water?"

"Sure."

"Good, because that's all I've got."

Adam went into the kitchen. He found a bag of cheap generic popcorn and tossed it into the microwave. While it was popping, he poured some water, added ice, then took the glasses into the living room. Phil accepted his without thanks.

"Damn. Another of those hanging deaths," said Phil. "Got a guy here visiting who's looking into that. Asked me about ghosts. Old-time correspondent and client. I've sold him a bunch of books."

"Oh?" said Adam.

He went and got the popcorn.

"Jeez. This was a nasty one, too."

"Spare me the details."

"Sure. So I'm supposed to get local history books and stuff. Shouldn't be hard. I'll just go over to the Lane County Museum and check with the Historical Society."

"Can't he do that?" said Adam, putting the DVD into the player.

"I want to get there first and find stuff for him. He's a good client and I want to impress him. Then I'll mention that he might want to go, too."

"Sly."

"Hey, hey."

"So I hear that the Animal House Bar is supposed to be opening next month. You oughta make your comeback then. 'Course that's one heck of a long trip."

"What, downtown?"

"No. A comeback from the comedy cemetery. Heh heh."

Adam made a high hat sound. "Ouch."

"Just joking. You're happy in your retirement."

"Yes."

"Ready to fire up *House of Wax*?"

"Sure."

As the music swelled and the movie began, Phil dug into the big plastic bowl of popcorn.

"Hey! This isn't butter!"

"Fuck you, Phil."

"Hey hey."

Later, after the movie, when Phil was gone, Adam read the article about the new death. He ran a trembling hand through his gray, thinning hair.

Then he put the paper down, sighed deeply and went to his study to be with his own noose.

8

The day after the ghost tour, Geoffrey Bullfinch dropped in on Maddy. She'd invited him over to talk. They had coffee outside in the deck chairs. It was a sunny fall day, a bit crisp in the morning, but warming up nicely.

"Your son is very bright," he said, once they'd settled in. "Very inquisitive."

"He's a bit autistic," said Maddy. "Very mild."

"They used to call that Asperger's syndrome, right?"

"Yes, as a matter of fact. How did you know that?"

"I've lived a long life. It's not the first time I've encountered the condition, nor I suspect will it be the last. He controls it well. I was hoping you might be willing to spare him a few hours while I'm in town. My research will require some assistance, and he seems to have a flair for the mysterious. I'd be willing to pay for his services, of course."

He smiled. She thought he looked a bit like the older David Niven.

Maddy didn't answer right away. She thought about Skylar, the way his face had lit up when the dowsing rods reacted. The way the "ghost club" at work seemed to ignite his interest and light his eyes. He so seldom reacted strongly to things.

"And you're a private detective?" Bullfinch said.

Maddy smiled. "That's right. I used to be a parole officer. Got tired of that and went into business for myself."

"And you get jobs from the police."

"Well, my boyfriend is a captain."

"I would be interested in contracting your services as well.

The best source of information in cases like these is the family, the crime scenes, the neighbors and friends. Anything you could find out would be helpful, and you are local—they are more likely to speak to you."

"Exactly what sort of research are you doing, Mr. Bullfinch?"

"Call me Geoffrey, please. Mr. Bullfinch is what they call me at the DMV, or the bank."

Maddy nodded, waiting.

"The organization I work for monitors strange occurrences," he said finally. "Without going into detail, the hanging deaths here in Eugene triggered interest, and I was selected to investigate because such events fall in line with my expertise, and because I was free and not too far away."

"Are there many of you?" Maddy asked.

"A few. They are a remarkable group. In any case, as I'm certain you have already gathered, I do not believe these deaths are suicide. I'm also not certain they are murders, at least not of a standard nature. I would like nothing better than to be proven wrong, but for that to happen I am going to have to spend a great deal of time poking around, reading, taking notes... Your help with the legwork would free me to do more of that—and Skylar's assistance would help cut down on the time."

"Those are among Sky's favorite pastimes," Maddy said. "Research. Discovery. It's hard sometimes to know what will interest him, but when something does..."

The afternoon was beautiful. Daylight Savings Time was supposed to go away over the weekend, but in the meantime they'd just been treated to a glorious sunset. Clouds scudded along in an azure sky like serene spirits above the buttes and rivers that defined the South Willamette countryside. Maddy lived on the other side of the Willamette River in a fairly respectable trailer park. She had a nice view of Skinner Butte, named after Eugene Skinner, the city's founder.

They sipped their coffee for a moment in silence, then turned as one as a new sound invaded the silence. First, there was the wiry squeak of wheels. Then a bike ground its tires on gravel and, in a moment, Skylar appeared.

"Well, speak of the devil."

When he saw that his mom had a visitor, Sky didn't smile or react. He stopped and took off his helmet.

"I thought you'd come," Skylar said, nodding to Bullfinch, but with no inflection in his voice.

"You guys talked last night, right?" said Maddy.

"We did," said Skylar.

"Sky, Mr. Bullfinch has a proposition. He wants you to work with him."

"Oh? For money?"

"Yes. Through me, so I'll supervise. He's doing an exploration on the possibility that these deaths lately in town—we've talked about them, and you've heard about them, right?"

"Yes. Of course."

"That they might have something to do with… ghosts. Mr. Bullfinch—Geoffrey—you are free to speak to my son. I'll be here, of course."

"Of course."

Sky sat down after parking and locking his bike. A slight curve turned up one corner of his mouth, almost imperceptible. "Ghosts. Wow."

"Yes. I'm a collector of myths and legends. I've been studying the paranormal for a very long time, and I know a lot of odd things. As I mentioned last night, I also work for an organization very interested in the strange and the unexplained. We try to help people with what we know and what we can do."

Sky nodded. "Sure."

"So I'm here in this case not just to investigate but to help. Much as your mother helps people. If she agrees, she's going to be working the families of the case… the families of the people who've died."

"You mean as a private detective?"

"Yes."

"Sounds good. My mom could use some money. I could use some money."

"And you will be paid."

"Great."

"What I'd need you to do would be along the lines of acting as a research assistant. I don't know the local libraries, and it might take a lot of reading and searching to piece together anything useful."

"Oh, yeah. I can do that," Skylar said. "I already do that."

"So do you agree?"

"Sure, but… it's not just me who's interested in ghosts. It's my friends, too. It's my ghost hunting club. Would you pay them too?"

"Hmm. Would I have to go and speak to all their parents individually."

"No. We have a treasury. Pay the treasury, and we can all help you."

"Then, of course, I accept. Your mother and I will work out the details on that. I'm in need of all the help I can get, but full disclosure… it's your services I especially need."

"Why is that?"

"As I mentioned, I've been doing this sort of thing for a long time. I have colleagues who I wish might be here to advise me and join in directly, but they are otherwise engaged." He coughed and sipped the dregs of his coffee. "I believe that you are a very special young man."

Maddy's eyebrows rose, but she held her silence.

"I saw how you reacted last night," Bullfinch said. "I believe that you exhibit some signs of being clairvoyant. Like a sensitive."

Skylar almost smiled. "I am, of course."

Maddy was taken aback.

"You know this? Why didn't you tell me?"

"You never asked." He looked thoughtful. "But mother, I did tell you about Mr. Aardvark."

"Sky, he was your imaginary friend. Lots of children have imaginary friends."

"Oh, Mr. Aardvark wasn't just imaginary! You acted as though you believed me when I told you."

"Well, of course I did… I mean, parents humor their children about that sort of thing and…" She looked up and saw that Bullfinch was smiling paternally.

"So are you interested in working with Mr. Bullfinch?"

Skylar actually smiled. "I certainly am."

"Well, Geoffrey," she said. "Looks like we should talk terms." She glanced over at Sky.

He seemed about as delighted as he ever got—but still, oddly thoughtful.

9

"So then, Mr. Norse," said Maddy. "Can you tell me about this Noose Club?"

"Sure," said Jim Norse. He was a man of about forty-five, with a trim beard, a bald spot behind short brown hair, and a sincere expression. He wore a suit and a tie, loosened at the neck. The city was on a mid-day break, and he was clearly making the most of it. They were at a nice Italian-style coffee bar in an old building. A huge picture of an Italian nobleman looking very espressoed-up watched them from the far wall behind a display of fancy cappuccino cups for sale.

"I bought this house. I was exploring the attic—the former owners left a lot of junk up there—and in an old trunk, along with other antiques, there was this noose. I should say, an *old* noose... an old hangman's noose."

"How did you know it was a hangman's noose?"

"I didn't at first, it was just a feeling I got from it. Then I researched it. It was the style of knot they used here back in the day for formal hangings."

"As opposed to lynchings."

Norse gave a morbid nod. "Yeah."

"Go on. You found this noose?"

"Yes. Well, I got very interested in what kind of story it might have attached to it. I'm interested in the history of this area, and the noose just exacerbated that, I guess. I was already in city government. A politician, and politicians—well, they meet a lot of people. I guess I talked about the noose pretty often. Before I knew it, I was talking to Fred."

"Fred Evans. The most recently hanged man."

"That's right. Fred Evans. And he got this look on his face."

"You know," he said, "That's very much like what happened to me. Only I found my noose in a garage sale. And I just had to have it. I don't know why."

"Turned out there was a loose collection of guys who'd all found similar old nooses. Some found them in basements and some found them in estate sales. Plenty of those around here. We all were interested in history, so we started to get together for informal meetings. You know, bowling or golf or just to have a beer. A loose social club, but with a thread."

"Or a noose."

"Yes."

"How long has this Noose Club been going on?"

"Oh, about eight or nine years. I got in about three ago. And there's one more member who joined just a couple of years ago."

"And then, a few months ago, these suicides started."

Norse shook his head. "No. No, I refuse to believe that any of my friends killed themselves. I believe they were murdered." He had an intense expression on his face.

"The doors were locked from the inside in each case, Mr. Norse."

Norse shook his head. "I know… and I think I know why."

"There's something you haven't told the police."

"Yes. And that's why I'm talking to you. We've met on a few other occasions over the years."

"You remember?"

"Yes. And I'm a good judge of people. That's an important trait in a politician." He cleared his throat. "Anyway, I had a positive reaction to you. I have a gut feeling I can trust you. And I can't always trust the police or too many people in the political field. If you know what I mean."

"Oh, I do, I do."

"Good." He leaned forward with great sincerity. "Madrigal."

"Please. Call me Maddy."

"I was almost hanged the other night by my noose."

She blinked. "You mean, murdered?

"Yes."

"Did you see the killer?"

"No. Because I think it's some sort of supernatural force."

"I guess the question I most want answered, then," Maddy said, "is do you still have that noose, and if so... why?"

10

A shiver ran through Geoffrey Bullfinch.

He looked around.

Nothing behind him. As he walked along the shady path leading to the high school, he could have sworn someone was following him. The rustle of dead leaves. The acrid stench of a dead thing. The touch of cool air on his neck.

He shivered again and proceeded toward the school.

It was a huge, Gothic monstrosity of the old sort. The kind that Bullfinch frankly preferred. The one-level modern school wonders really had the personality of fleas. This one, though, with its gables and eye-like windows… it spoke to him.

He climbed the steep steps, signed in at the office, and then went down a hall, turned left and into another to the room Skylar had instructed.

There, waiting for him, would be the scheduled meeting of the Skinner High School Ghost Hunters Assembly. He wasn't sure what might come of the meeting, but as Sherlock Holmes had taken advantage of his irregulars, Bullfinch was ready to take advantage of any resource, so long as no one was endangered.

He found the room easily enough, mostly by the mild roar of conversation from within. He knocked on the door politely.

"Might I come in?" he said.

"Mr. Bullfinch. Yes, of course!" said Skylar. "He is here."

Bullfinch stepped in and took in the room quickly. Artwork and posters lined the walls, maps (the type that roll up into a tube like an old-fashioned film screen) hung on the walls.

"Thank you for inviting me, Sky. What a nice classroom."

"Not really," said a girl in a black hoodie and black makeup, slouching at her desk. "It's a math class."

Bullfinch widened his eyes. "Oh my, yes. I hated math when I was young."

"But you're so—well—smart." Skylar said. He looked concerned. And Bullfinch knew that Sky probably did well at math.

"There are different kinds of smart though, aren't there? Also different types of math. Symbols, and patterns, those fascinate me. It's the dreary equations of physics—the endless efforts to take what is amazing, and simplify it to an equation—that I find baffling."

He glanced around the room, then winked at Skylar. "Speaking of different, did you know that I have Second Sight?"

He didn't, of course. And no one in the room likely knew what the term meant, but it attracted all their attention. Suddenly all twenty-one students in the ghost hunting club were very interested in their guest speaker.

"You did not tell me that," said Sky.

"Second Sight," said the girl in black. "What's that?"

"Let's get settled in, shall we? Bullfinch said. "Then I'll be happy to explain."

"Sure," Sky said. "We brought in a podium for you. They usually use it for student gatherings or pep rallies."

Bullfinch hefted his valise onto a desk, but looked thoughtfully at the chair beside it. "I wonder if I might just sit and speak? I'd like to keep this informal, and I've been on my feet most of the day."

Sky looked surprised.

"Let him sit, you idiot!" said the girl in the black hoodie.

"Sure," Sky said.

Bullfinch lowered himself carefully into the stiff-backed chair. Thankfully, it wasn't a middle school—the chairs were more or less adult in size. Just not particularly comfortable. He got right to it.

"I believe I met a few of you at the ghost tour the other night.

That was remarkable, was it not?"

There was a bobbing of heads.

"I didn't go," said the girl in black.

"Well, you are here and that's what's important. Might I ask your name?"

She sat up, squinting at him. "Why do you want to know?"

"You remind me of someone. I'm just wondering if you are related. Please, don't think I'm prying. If you don't want to…"

"It's Natosha Peters. And that's 'Natosha' with an 'O'," she spat defiantly, looking around at the others.

"It's a very beautiful name, and that is a classic spelling—very old. I'd have to look it up, but I believe that may be the Bulgarian spelling, as opposed to the Russian."

"Yeah!" said a gangly guy. "Like Boris and Natasha."

"Shut *up*, you jerk."

"Hey guys, please," said Sky, cutting off the impending argument impatiently. "Mr. Bullfinch is here to talk to us about something important."

"I am," Bullfinch agreed. "And I need help. I asked your name, Natosha, for a very important reason. Do you have Second Sight?"

"Huh?"

"I sense that's why you are here. You were drawn here. You may all have this talent. I believe Skylar does."

"Skylar can't even do *first* sight," said the gangly kid.

"Oh really?" Bullfinch said. "I wonder if that outburst was wise," said Bullfinch. "You see, I sense someone here… someone here is of Gypsy blood. Gypsies know the way of the curse, and I sense she is angry with you…"

"You bet I am, Castonetti!" said Natosha. Then, as suddenly as she'd spoken, she caught herself. "Hey. How did you… Well, okay, now you know."

"Wow!" said a boy in the back.

"Cool," said another.

"Amazing," said a girl.

"Natosha. You never told us! That's way awesome."

Natosha looked puzzled, but not displeased.

"All of that and more, I believe," Bullfinch added. "The *travelers*, as I sometimes call them in my books, are more in touch with the ways of the past, and things unseen. Perhaps that's why you are in the ghost hunters club."

"Maybe," said Natosha.

"In any case, what I have to say here many of you doubtless already know, but I think that I bring two different slants that are appropriate for this group and this situation. I hope to get your help."

"Sure."

"Cool."

"First, I should introduce myself. My name is Geoffrey Bullfinch. I specialize in the study of myths, legends, and folklore. It is my belief that there is truth behind most of the old stories— even if sometimes it's only a psychological truth. Ghosts are an important part of this. Ghosts are the spirits, souls, or some sort of psychic remnant of deceased humans, though there are some tales of ghost animals, who linger in the material world, manifesting themselves in different ways.

"Here's an interesting thing you may not know about ghosts. The English word ghost is derived from an Old Norse word for 'fury'. In all cultures, part of the reason folks are afraid of ghosts is that, as often as not, they are 'vengeful'. They've got chips on their shoulders. They are spirits stuck here who want to hurt people. If only scare them."

He paused for a moment. He'd asked Skylar for a glass of water to be on the desk, and sure enough, there it was. He took a sip, and looked at the students. They were all transfixed.

"It looks as though we might just have a vengeful ghost here in Eugene. Anyone have any idea why?"

"My dad…" said a boy, who clammed up immediately. "Uhm…well… Uhm."

"Please, go ahead."

"My dad says it's all nonsense. We've all heard the stories. The newspaper and the news guy on TV say there's no way anyone could have murdered those guys who got hanged, but my dad says there's always a 'logical explanation'."

"Perhaps the wild is hidden."

There was a stillness in the room. Every eye and ear was fixed on Bullfinch.

"Friends, let me tell you what I think is the truth about ghosts."

11

"A ghost?"

"Or a demon," said Jim Norse. "Or some sort of vengeful spirit. Who knows? I'm not a superstitious man. Never have been. This experience, though, and the whole business with the Noose Club, it's freed up my thinking somewhat."

Maddy sipped at her coffee. It had cooled, but it was still good, sweet and bitter at the same time with enough milk to make it smooth.

She scribbled something in her notebook.

"You sound like a man who prefers evidence."

"Oh, I am. I used to be a trial lawyer." Jim Norse finally smiled.

"What happened to make you change your mind?"

"The other night..." He leaned forward. He'd grown noticeably paler. "I almost hung myself. And I heard...experienced... the thing. Trying to make me hang myself. I have no explanation for what it was, or how it could *be*, but I believe it was some sort of malevolent spirit."

"You're sure it wasn't a delusion?"

"I'm sound psychologically, I assure you."

"No offense, but that's exactly what an unsound person would say. This fascination with the noose, it doesn't sound healthy."

"I suppose not, particularly hearing about it from the 'outside-in' as you are. Still, I don't believe this is a psychological aberration. I felt something physical. Whatever happened, whatever it was that influenced me, it had some sort of power behind it."

"You mean like…what do they call them? Poltergeists?"

"Yes. Although most recorded poltergeists are psychic emanations, and they generally involve troubled teenagers."

"You know a lot about poltergeists for a local politician."

"I'm curious, wouldn't you be? I mean, if something like this happened to you? I've done some research on my own, though not much has come of it."

"What exactly do you remember?"

She took notes as he spoke.

He'd gone up to his study in the attic. He had not locked the door. He'd held the noose for a while and found himself putting it around his neck. The next thing he knew, the end of the noose was looped over a rafter, and he was standing on a chair. He'd sensed something profoundly evil in the room with him the room. Then he had clearly felt—or heard?—a command to kick away the chair.

He'd almost done it.

He'd caught himself just in time, and regained his balance. He'd reached up to take the noose off of the rafter, and suddenly he'd felt a force working on the chair, moving it from under his feet. With all his strength he'd pushed himself up, freeing the noose just as the chair toppled, spilling him to the ground. He'd hit hard, and for just a moment he'd lost consciousness. When he'd awakened, the presence had already left. The noose lay on the floor beside him, and the door to downstairs was locked!

"And you are sure you hadn't locked it yourself."

"Positive. I never do that," said Norse. "Why would I?"

Maddy tapped her pad with her pen.

Something was wrong here. Something weird—and not in a supernatural way. She'd read far too many stories and books where what seemed to be supernatural at first turned out to be explainable, and her courses in criminology had been full of people who drank blood, thinking they were vampires, and were not. People who thought they were werewolves and killed other people by tearing out their throats with their teeth. People who believed that they were possessed who turned out to merely be psychotics.

And the locked room thing. That was Houdini territory.

"Tell me about the other members of your organization."

"You mean the Noose Club? The 'Loose Noosers'?"

"That's right. You must be pretty upset now, all of you."

"Of course."

"How many members?"

"Thirteen."

"Ah. And so many dead now, from the same cause."

"Don't you have most of the facts about that from the families who hired you?"

"I don't have all the necessary information. I didn't get to interview any of the victims. How could the families have known? Does your wife know? There have to be secrets. For instance, did you have some sort of secret initiation rite?"

"Heavens no! What do you think we are, Satanists?"

"Never suggested that. Clubs, though, tend to acquire rules."

"Like I said, it's a loose aggregation."

"And you play cards and bowl and talk about nooses."

"Yeah. We get along pretty well."

"Are there other people who know about your club?"

"Sure. Not that many. It's not a secret though. Our wives and families certainly know."

"Yes. And no one disapproves?"

"What do you think? Of course our wives didn't care much for it at first. After a while, they saw we were just a friendly group who needed to help each other unwind. We all have stressful jobs."

She smiled. "Aren't all jobs?"

"I guess."

"And your wife still approves—with all the hangings?"

Norse shrugged.

"One more question," said Maggie. She'd just had a brainstorm. "Of all the surviving members, who would you say was the angriest?"

His brow furrowed. "Angriest?"

"Yes. You know. Who would you say is most unhappy?"

"You mean, like, someone who would want to kill the rest of us?"

"Oh no! Not at all! I'm just shaking the tree a little here and seeing what falls out."

Norse was thoughtful.

Then he nodded.

"I guess that would be Adam."

12

The sky outside the window had darkened. A wind had risen, and bare tree branches scratched at a few of the window panes. From the few open windows, the scent of rain floated in.

No one got up to close them.

They were all concentrating on Geoffrey Bullfinch's words.

"We are all living, thinking beings. Complex organisms living in social colonies of mutual support, like bees—but less organized. Let me ask you a simple question. Hands up on this one. Ever been sitting alone studying, or strolling in a shady park... and then have the feeling that someone is staring at you? You turn around, *all* the way around, mind you, and there *is* someone staring at you?"

Hands shot into the air. One for each student. Even Skylar put his hand up.

"Okay, these people who've been staring at you for whatever reason—not important why... they aren't in your area of vision, not even your peripheral vision. So how did you know that someone was staring at you?"

"Some sort of psychic power that all humans possess?" volunteered a girl, looking fascinated but nonetheless nervous.

"Maybe there's an eye in the back of our head we don't know about!" said a big kid.

"Oh, you mean, like this one!"

Slowly, Bullfinch took off his fedora, placed it on the desk and started parting the hair on the back of his head.

The reaction was shock and chaos.

"No! Please."

"Oh my God!"

"I gotta get outta here."

Natosha said, "Guys, he's joking!"

Bullfinch grinned and pointed. "Gotcha!"

The room broke out into laughter.

"So you see, what we investigators have to face is a huge amount of superstition. That is, people *want* to believe this. But the question is, why? You see, I'm not really a psychic investigator. I just play one on TV."

More laughter.

"Seriously. I collect legends, myths, and folklore. Ghosts are a part of all this, so I do research them at times. Believe me, there are many more proofs of the existence of psychic powers and strange abilities in human beings than simple hauntings and intuitions. It's my opinion, from my study of ancient myths and legends, that modern men and women, that is humans of the last two thousand years, have lost a good deal of the psychic, or mental, abilities that our ancestors took for granted.

"In myths and legends we hear of gods, demi-gods, monsters, and oracles. I suppose you've read the work of Rick Riordan, many of you?"

Several of those gathered nodded and smiled.

"Pretty good." one girl said. "I like the movies too…"

"A bit fanciful, but an interesting way to keep the old stories alive," Bullfinch said. "My family has been recording and researching those stories for a very long time. I am reasonably certain that if you check your library, you'll find a copy of *Bullfinch's Mythology* on the shelves. In any case, I feel that we are all psychic, to a point, and therefore can be called 'supernatural' beings in the parlay of modern science. I am not here to tear down modern science. I am merely suggesting that its methods have blinded it to a lot of amazing things.

"But back to ghosts. Ghosts, I believe, are energy creatures. They exist because, while they were alive, they generated sufficient psychic energy of a certain type that cannot be removed from this particular plane. Like a photograph, or a memory that many people can share. More often than not, violence, anger—extreme emotion—provides the catalyst. Do you remember what I mentioned before?

"Yes, sir," said Skylar. "That the word ghost is derived from the Norse term for 'fury'."

"Well done, Sky. So, what you have is a dense pack of energy, complex, connected to a place transmitted by the energy generated by the mind of a human being. Result: When the human being dies, there is a sort of residue. Sometimes these psychic impressions are simply amorphous and shifting. They can also appear malevolent—even intelligent. Intelligent, I believe, in an artificial manner. Not a true intelligence, more of a machine intelligence. An A.I. if you will."

"Yeah. There are people *alive* without 'true intelligence'—must be harder for a ghost," said Natosha.

Everyone laughed.

"Exactly," said Bullfinch. "Of course, not every instance of haunting is fueled by anger. There are all sorts of emotions powerful enough to leave their mark, reasons something might be left behind after death."

"So they aren't dead souls," said Sky.

"A soul implies a maker, I believe. It's not a term I use, because, even though I deal in gods and goddesses, I myself have found no actual solid existence of the existence of one."

"No God, no Devil, right?"

"I'm not going to say definitively that there is no God. That would be as foolish as stating the opposite. The Devil though… Demons. Possession. You know, again, I've found no empirical evidence. There is plenty of evidence of psychic occurrence and mental illness, and a lot of those occurrences have been labeled as possession over the centuries. Plenty of evidence of transcendental and religious experiences as well, though again—not backed up by research. The human brain is a strange and mysterious thing.

"I'll give you an example. There is a famous book that I've read many times called *The Bicameral Mind*. This book posits that there is a reason why we have all our myths and legends. And that is quite simply, the ancient mind worked quite differently from our own—a thing we are already aware of. This book, however, suggests that ancient men were what contemporary psychologists might call 'schizophrenic'. That is, they heard voices in their minds, and the voices told them to do things.

"If you were poor Zoberba the shepherd, maybe the voice told you to offer one of your sheep in sacrifice to Zeus. But now, what if you had a lot more power? What if you were King Herod in Judea, and you heard a voice saying *kill all the babies born in the last few days in this land*. Well, now that's history, isn't it?

"But that was about two to five thousand years ago. Let's say forty thousand years ago in ancient Babylon these leaders started hearing their voices, and these voices told the people they had names. *My name is Zoroaster*, or *My name is Imhotep*, or—switching to ancient Egypt—*My name is Ra*.

"If you heard the voice of a god in your head, wouldn't you sit up and take notice? I would."

Everyone laughed.

"So they had voices that said they were Zeus or Odin, up north?" a chubby boy said.

"Exactly. I mean, take a look at our friends, the aborigines in Australia. They see and think things differently than most of us, don't they?"

"You really believe this?" said Natosha.

Bullfinch chuckled. "I believe nothing until I have witnessed it, or been convinced. In this particular case, I'm just explaining one fascinating theory."

"It's weird."

"Well, don't you think there are those who might believe *you* are weird? Don't you think we're all weird?"

Everyone laughed again.

"I'm going to assume that, with all the news stories, Internet posts, and television shows available, that you all know a bit about insanity. About psychosis and schizophrenia and all the ills of the mind. In fact, we all have to work very hard in this modern world to stay sane.

"Ultimately, the point that I'm trying to make is, if you stay sane, if you stay firm in your conviction of the basic tenets of reason in the universe, you're safe." He paused and looked around. "There is nothing to be afraid of!"

"You should have told me that the other night when we had that ghost walk in the cemetery. I almost crapped my pants," said one of the students.

This time, it was nervous laughter.

"Any time a human mind deals with the unknown it gets nervous or frightened. I take it, by the way, that we are all human here tonight?"

No one disagreed.

"In fact, there's an old word that's not used very much that I find very handy when I speak about ghosts. It's 'numinous'."

"Numerous?"

"No. Numinous. It is a feeling you get. I'll give you an example. If there's a goat in the room with you, you get a certain feeling. You feel, well, that's unusual, there being a goat in the room and all, but it's not beyond my imagination. Now…and here's where it gets weird…suppose someone enters that same room and swears to God Almighty that there is a 'ghost' in the next room?"

"I'd be kinda spooked," said a student.

"Exactly. A bit of a shiver from some ancient part of you, a part you don't usually use. That is what numinous means. It's a sensation that I believe our ancient ancestors experienced more often than we do. Imagine that you're an ancient man—or woman—sitting in the dark and the damp, feeling sorry for yourself. Suddenly there is this great bright light rising up from the east. It's warm, and as you watch it, you begin to feel better. It feels magical, and, of course it is. It is the bringer of life. It is a God. It is the Sun. Hence you have Apollo and his chariot—the myth, that is, and all the many Sun gods.

"What I'm saying is that all of this awareness of the supernatural is hard-wired in us all, to different degrees. That's why many of us are sensitive to the existence of these renegade residuals of psychic energy. Ghosts!"

"You're saying this is all a kind pseudo-science?" said Natosha.

"Yes, but that word is used by more traditional scientists to describe what their systems cannot detect or understand, or to describe things that defy rational investigation. It's like what Hamlet says to Horatio. 'There are things, Horatio, not dreamt of in your philosophy.'"

"Yeah, but Hamlet's dad was the real thing! And he was in hell!" said Natosha.

"Ghosts, my dear, are always most real in fiction!"

Again, laughter.

"I believe it is important that you were interested enough to start a ghost hunters club. I believe these things stretch the mind. Open us to new possibilities. More to the point, though, in this situation we have a current Eugene ghost story on our hands."

"The Hanging Ghost!" said Natosha.

"Is that what folks are calling him? Have any of you ever heard, perhaps from your parents, or teachers, or even grandparents, of any previous mentions of this 'Hanging Ghost,' or 'The Noose Ghost'? I prefer to check with the general public since it is with folk that I find folklore."

"Yeah," said a boy. "My dad was talking about that this morning at breakfast. He says he remembers his dad up in Coburg talk about a ghost that haunts the sight of its gallows."

"Good. I'll check with you later."

There were a few more stories. Bullfinch dutifully scribbled them down.

"And finally—I have a very important question. Is there a man anywhere in your neighborhoods who lives by himself, doesn't go out much, and, in short, seems what you might call 'creepy'?"

"Oh yeah!" said Natosha. "There is for sure."

13

Eugene, Oregon, is a city built on two rivers, the Willamette and
the McKenzie. These are two mighty rivers that take water
from the Cascade Mountains and the smaller Coast Range to the
West. As a result, when Eugene Skinner and his fellow pioneers
first came into the place, they discovered that the area around the
rivers flooded nearly every spring, spilling out a massive amount
of water until they hit the surrounding hills and taller buttes.

This flooding discouraged many settlers, ideal as the terrain
was in many other ways. They made camp and built up settle-
ments in areas such as Harrisburg and Pleasant Hill, Cottage
Hill and Goshen.

Eugene Skinner, however, was a tenacious fellow.

There was a pleasant butte by the Willamette, and Skinner
built houses on the upsweep there, where the spring waters did
not reach. Then, he brought in engineers to figure out what to do
about the floods.

"Skinner's Folly" they called Eugene, Oregon.

By the time Oregon became a state in 1859, a state without
slaves, to the dismay of the South, a situation that helped to pre-
cipitate the American Civil War, Eugene was starting to build on
drier and drier land.

And flat lands. Thousands of years of flooding had flattened
large stretches. When the University of Oregon established a
track and field program they found their track area so flat and
popular, Eugene earned a new nickname "Track Town."

Today one of the varieties of pizza it serves is "Track Town
Pizza"

In the early '70s the University of Oregon runner Steve Prefontaine distinguished himself and his track coach, Bill Bowerman, with a remarkable set of victories. Bowerman, at the time, was perfecting a new sort of athletic shoe. Another man, Phil Knight, was attending business school at the same time, and he recognized the brilliance of Bowerman's product, combined with the marketability of Prefontaine's appeal. Knight started the Nike sports brand and never looked back, except to shower the University of Oregon and Stanford with funding.

Steve Prefontaine, alas, died young in a car accident near Lakewood Golf Course.

Just south of the Willamette River to the immediate west of Skinner's Butte is one of the oldest areas of Eugene. This area is called, simply, The Whitaker. Maddy ran over what she knew of the area as she drove. She had a lead, and she needed to try and run it down before her source clammed up.

Some years ago, the Whitaker neighborhood had been called "Felony Flats". It got the name because it was close to both the Eugene Mission and the train tracks, which regularly imported transients riding on freight trains, and because of that had a large population of undesirables. As a young parole officer, Maddy had been no stranger to the Whitaker. It was, in a word, funky. Old two- and three-story creaky houses, both Gothic and bungalows, sided its streets, covered in ivy and moss and shaded by ancient trees.

Now, though, crime had mostly moved south and east and the Whitaker was safer. Of course, it had never been *that* dangerous, not when you compared it to the slums of larger cities. Just shady.

It had not been gentrified—it retained its funky charm. Restaurants and stores had moved in, wine rooms, and most importantly, it had become the center for an explosion of Northwest beer brewing. Starting with Ninkasi, most of the area brewers either had brewing stations, tasting rooms, or pubs in the area.

As Maddy got out of her car beneath a large oak, the air was rich with the smell of fresh hops. She smiled.

She liked beer. Not as much as Bill or Hildy did, but she liked it, and was proud of her home town for its contribution to killing the Budweiser grip that companies like Anheuser-Busch had on America's vital beer money.

She checked the address again. 1346 2nd Street.

The house was an old pile indeed. Gothic in design, it was three stories high with gables, taller than it was wide. A rotten wooden gate opened onto a path through a tangled garden, leading to a porch badly in need of painting.

Maddy climbed the steps carefully and knocked on the door.

She had to pound a few more times before she got a response. There was no doorbell.

"Yes?" said a small voice behind the door.

"Mr. Even?"

"That's right."

"My name is Madrigal Harper. I'm a private detective. I wonder if I can ask you a few questions?"

The door opened. A white-haired man of about sixty peered out. He wore glasses, had a scruffy beard and a crop of ragged hair—not long, but not neat.

"Questions? About what?"

"Sorry to bother you, but I've been hired to put together some information. Hired by members and families of the Noose Club. They say you are a member."

"Oh my. Yes. Come in." Sheepishly, he opened the door and stepped aside. "If you move that stack of papers you can sit in the kitchen chair. I can get you a glass of water if you like. No ice, I'm afraid."

"I'm fine."

"You're with the police?"

"No. But your honest answers will help the police and spare them a trip."

"Oh. Good. I was expecting the police." He smiled. "You're much nicer than the police. Glad it worked out this way."

She moved the papers to the floor and sat down. He did the same with a second pile of papers and sat as well.

He wore a ratty t-shirt, a stained bathrobe and a pair of sweatpants that looked like they'd been old in the '70s. Despite all of this, Maddy could tell that, once upon a time, this guy hadn't been bad looking.

"Good. I like to simplify things. How long have you lived in Eugene, Mr. Even?"

"Off and on for about thirty-five years. Last twenty, mostly on."

"And how did you become a member of the Noose Club?"

"Easy! This house is as old as sin, as you can see. When I moved here a few years ago... I used to live in the South Hills in a nicer place, but then I... well... I needed to umm..." He smiled. "Let's just say I had to rearrange my finances. So when that happened I found this place on the cheap. I'm an entertainer. I can sing. I can dance. I had some money. I got a good price because some old people died in here. Lots of old people. I think they buried them in the back. Sure smells like it. They left lots of antique furniture, closets and chests. Anyway, a couple years ago, I was looking to sell some of what's here, looking through an old chest. I bet you can guess what I found inside."

"A noose?"

He nodded. "A really old noose."

"May I see it?"

"Can you wait a bit? I promise to show it to you, but I'm in a talking mood. I don't have much of anyone to talk to. You're here. Here's my talk. You got me. Take it from me. It's pretty much like all those other nooses."

"How did you get into the Noose Club?"

"I have this weird friend, Phil. He sells books. He knows lots of people, and he was visiting. He's got lots of comics. Sometimes I go and buy comics from him.

"So Phil, he tells me about this guy comin' to ask about books on Eugene history. And the guy's all excited. He's got noose news, he says. Can you imagine that? Noose news. Up here in the Northwest, you'd think it would be Moose News. Ha! So, me, I think, shit. I need new friends. And I like my noose. It's— umm—comforting in a really weird way. And interesting. I knew exactly what that guy was talking about."

"And who was that?'

"He's on the Eugene Council. Cool friend to know, you got a pothole in your street. Know what I mean?"

"Indeed I do! So that would be Jim Norse?"

"Yeah."

"He suggested I speak to you, since you were both intelligent and the most recent member of the Club."

"Oh yeah. You know what, Maddy? I'm talkin' and I like talkin'. I gotta talk now so listen to me. That Club helped me a lot. We played cards, we had picnics, we went bowling, we went out drinking beer. I was almost a shut-in, I gotta say, I was get-ting sadder and sadder. Still sad, but hey—life is sad, right? Com-edy is hard. Dying is easy."

"Comedy. Yes. Your friend said you're a comedian."

"Bingo!"

"Stand up. Used to do well. And you were in a lot of films?"

He chortled. "Yeah, they all had about a hundred bare female boobs and one male boob. Thankfully for the audience, not bare. Yours truly."

She laughed. "I gather you've retired."

"You gather correctly."

"What made you choose Eugene?"

"Love the place. I used to like to hike. It's far enough from L.A. and yet close enough to hop down if you need to. And far, far from Brooklyn."

"You're from New York City?"

"Nope. Brooklyn. And if you don't know the difference, then I'm not gonna explain."

"Yes. Come to think of it, you do have a bit of an accent."

"Gee. So I've wasted all that soap."

She laughed again. "You're funny."

"That's what they paid me for. Give me some good material, I can make a nice dress and wear it well."

"You should go out and do shows."

He shrugged.

She let it go. "So anyway you're in this Noose Club and…"

Suddenly there was a crash from an upper floor. Like a vase falling and smashing.

She glanced up.

"Cat," said Adam Even.

There was a screaming, that could have been another cat, and then some thumping.

"I've got far too many cats," said Adam Even, deadpan.

She thought she heard what could have been hissing, but it seemed to have a voice as well. Then, just a hiss. A cat's hiss surely.

He stood up. "Don't make me come up there!"

Silence.

He smiled and shrugged again. "Cats! Only the Chinese know what to do with them."

"Anyway, where was I?"

"The Noose Club…"

There was a knock on the door.

"Judas Priest, I'm a popular feller today," he said. "Excuse me?"

"Sure," said Maddy. "Sure."

She looked nervously up at the ceiling.

She realized the hairs at the back of her neck had risen.

14

Bullfinch followed Sky and the dark-haired girl Natosha down a rather run-down, but quiet street. It was Saturday, the two were out of school, and they had agreed to show him the one house that fit the description he'd offered up at their meeting. It was a pleasant day, and though he was less than certain they would encounter anything useful to the case, he was enjoying the fresh air.

"Nice neighborhood," he said. "And, did I see a pub back there, and something called Tiny Tavern?"

"Oh yeah," said Natosha. "Whitaker is a funky heaven for boozehounds. Beer and wine mostly, but you want whiskey, we got this weird Japanese country and western place that serves it in big glasses—or so my old man says."

"Yes," said Sky. "Every year they have this big block party down here. I don't know why they call it a block party because it's many more than one block. They have a lot of good food and live music."

"And beer, I'm guessing," Bullfinch said.

"Yeah. There are a lot of breweries down here. Every year my old man has a high old time," said Natosha.

Bullfinch made a mental note to listen for more mentions of Natosha's father. Could be a harmless love of spirits, but it could also be more.

Natosha had already identified her family's place, a sweet little townhouse off of Monroe near 2nd Street. She had grown up in the neighborhood and knew all about "The Whit".

"Okay," said Natosha. "This is the place."

"Wow. Munsters or Addams Family, what do you think, Nathosha?" said Sky

"Addams Family. You'll see."

They marched up the unpainted, splotchy deck to the porch. The door was imposing and equally in need of paint.

"You better knock, Mr. Bullfinch," said Natosha, suddenly very reserved and polite. "I think this guy might recognize me."

Bullfinch studied her for a moment, wondering what sort of mischief she feared the tenant might recognize her from, but he let it slide.

"Of course. I have knocked on many doors in my life, and this one looks particularly inviting in its odd way."

He went up and knocked.

There was the sound of footsteps and the door opened.

The man was half as Natosha had described him. Disheveled, yes. Creepy? Well, not particularly.

The man in the doorway smiled. "Welcome," he said. "I have to say, I'm not used to receiving so many callers... Is it my birthday? I think I paid my taxes."

"Good afternoon," said Bullfinch. "My name is Bullfinch. I'm in town doing some research, and these young folks were kind enough to guide me to your door. I've been told that you might be a member of the Noose Club?"

"Bullfinch!" the strong voice echoed through the house.

Bullfinch started, turning to Sky and raising an eyebrow.

"Well, great minds think alike," the voice continued.

Bullfinch found himself confronted by the tall and beautiful form of Madrigal Harper. He was not sorry to see her... nor after his first startled reaction, was he particularly surprised.

"And look. My my, it's Siouxie Sue! And just how are the Banshees doing?" the man in the doorway asked, winking at Natosha.

"Adam," Maddy said, "This is my son, Skylar, his—friend? And this gentleman is our friend Geoffrey Bullfinch, who is helping us with our investigation."

"I'm glad to help, too." Adam Even said, holding out his hand.

Bullfinch shook it. "Maddy here has got me talkin', and lately getting me talking is like trying to get Howard Stern to shut up!"

They all laughed, even Natosha, who seemed a bit dismayed at the Siouxie reference.

"Come into my parlor," he said in a Peter Lorre imitation. "I am always a good host to those who wish… information. Soon Rick will come and give me my papers and I shall get on a plane and fly far, far from here! Heh heh."

He started chuckling.

"Creepy?" said Sky to Natosha.

"Bipolar."

They all went back to the parlor and Adam managed to clear enough horizontal surfaces to seat them all.

"Drink service, I fear, ended a few minutes ago."

"That's fine," Bullfinch assured him. "We won't be here long. I must say I do admire your house."

"A find. A steal. I'm a lucky guy. Right now, it doesn't suit my mood. Mostly though, it suits me to a cemetery T."

"It seems Adam is something of a comic," said Maddy.

"I got a few problems, yeah. Take my cats… please!"

Maddy looked a bit chagrined and looked up at the ceiling.

Bullfinch watched her, followed her gaze, and frowned. He sensed something—off—in the place, but could not put his finger on it.

Natosha looked a bit uncomfortable, but sat still and listened.

"Oh. Wait," said Skylar. "In films, did you go by the name of Adam Even?"

"Why yes!"

"I collect your films. And I got a tape of your '80s HBO show too. Very rare."

"Jeez, kid. I'll say. I ain't got one of those! But what's a nice young man like yourself doing with a bunch of cheesy comedy exploitation movies of dwindling quality?"

"Skylar!" said Maddy. "That's a very good question."

"Oh, Mom. Hildy likes him too. She helped me collect 'em.

You know how I like to collect stuff."

"Maddy, you really shouldn't be allowing the destruction of young minds. So here I am, the Jerry Lewis of Eugene. Hey, laydeeeeeeeee."

"Oh no. You're good! You must have improvised some of your lines in all the later films. You've got some zingers, as Bill says."

Adam put on a Billy Crystal "So nu!" face. "I did. You and your friends are very perceptive."

"One of our favorites is *Big Balls*, the bowling movie with the bearded ladies and you as the couch. Now that was funny."

"Skylar, you have a friend forever."

Adam seemed honestly taken aback, smiling.

"Well, now," Bullfinch said, bemused. "I'm afraid I'm lacking in the proper cultural details to follow much of this…"

"Adam Even was a comic who had a bit part in *National Lampoon's Animal House*," Maddy said. "It's a famous comedy filmed here and in Cottage Grove. The filmmakers found a dilapidated fraternity house and used that for exteriors and I think some interiors. It starred Donald Sutherland, John Vernon, but it also introduced new screen actors like Karen Allen and most of all John Belushi from *Saturday Night Live*. It was a surprise hit and they tried to do a sequel with different actors, including Adam Even in a bigger role. But things went wrong. Apparently one of the enigmas of the universe is how Hollywood gets anything done at all, considering how odd it is."

"Amen. Halleluiah! A member of the populace two thousand and so young… understands," Adam chuckled.

"I didn't say I understood, Mr. Even. Do you?"

"Hell no!"

Adam fell back into his chair, bent over and laughing. He seemed to be having a hard time speaking for a while.

Bullfinch noticed that Maddy was glaring at Skylar, who did not even seem to notice.

"I'm gonna have to talk to Hildy," said Maddy. "That's all I have to say."

"Hey, bring her over!" said Adam.

"Mr. Even. Would you sign my VHS boxes?"

"Sure, Sky. Sure." Adam wiped his eyes with his sleeve. "Yeah, come over whenever you want. Now, sorry, what more do you want to know about the Noose Club?"

"Well," said Maddy. "I guess I'm wondering how you feel about all that's been happening."

Adam drooped. "Oh. Right. Bring me down. I'll tell you how I feel. I knew a gal. And in the Seventies, she got murdered by the Son of Sam. I feel really bad. About five times as bad. And let me tell you, whatever you need to know, I'll tell you. I'm just happy to spill to you and not to the police."

"It may come to that."

He shrugged. "May not. Who knows." He shook his head. "Look, you know one of the reasons I retired?" He hit his chest lightly with a fist. "Bad ticker. I've enjoyed your visit, but I'm thinking if we don't postpone the rest of it, I may croak in front of your faces. And not dangling on a noose, either. Do you have any *immediate* questions?"

He was still smiling.

"I think we have enough for now. Bullfinch?"

"Perhaps I'll let Skylar ask a question or two."

Maddy seemed surprised, but she nodded.

"Sure. Shoot, kid." Adam said.

"Do you believe in ghosts, Mr. Even?"

"Absolutely. Never seen one, but I listen to… what's the name of it. Art Bell used to do it and now they got the guy George Noory who acts more credulous. Oh yeah. *Coast to Coast.* Late show. Sometimes I get insomnia. It helps me sleep. If I listen to that show for a couple of hours, I start sawing the logs."

Skylar nodded.

"Thanks. Over to you, Mr. Bullfinch."

"You've been here a while, albeit off and on, then," Bullfinch said.

"That's right."

"And you believe in ghosts."

"You bet. But I try to stay away from them, know what I mean?"

"Wise. In the time that you've been here... what would you say would be, in your opinion, the most haunted area in the town?"

"That would probably be the Eugene Hotel. It's called the *Old Eugene Hotel* now. It's across from the downtown post office."

"We saw that on the ghost tour. Apparently there used to be a brothel there."

Adam laughed. "I wouldn't know. Bit before my time. Any around now?"

"As a former law enforcement officer of the city of Eugene," said Maddy. "I assure you there isn't enough per capita income to warrant such an illegal place."

"Just strip bars."

"Just strip bars. I have a friend who practically lives in those. When he's not selling books."

"Oh. You know Philip Roman?" Bullfinch said, glancing up from his notes.

"Yeah!" said Adam. "One of my life's back-monkeys."

"It's a small world," Bullfinch said. He smiled. "I think that's all for now. You've been most helpful."

"And very entertaining," Maddy added.

"Glad to be of help, folks. And thanks for the memories!"

After they'd left, Adam moved the chairs back into place.

Glass broke somewhere above. He looked up. There was a yowling sound, wretched, and not unlike a cat.

He knew it was not a cat.

"Yeah, yeah. I'm coming, I'm coming. Hold onto your horns."

15

It was a nice place, out by Churchill High, in West Eugene, in a small shopping complex. Phil had suggested it because it was by one of his favorite conventional sit-down restaurants.

There was also an area in the back that could be rented for extra seating. So Ralphie liked that too.

They'd been open for a few days now, and while business wasn't great, it wasn't bad either. Now that they had a couple guys doing the food cart, they could focus on their real goal—their own restaurant.

"It's just a pizza joint!" Phil would say, the fuckin' asshole. It wasn't. It was a Jersey Pizza Parlor, like back home outside of Newark, where Ralphie and Lynn would go for their slices back when they were younger. You wanted, you could just cut and run with a quick box full, or if you had some time, sit and chew at a checkerboard tablecloth with a fake rose on it. You were hungrier? Shit, they had good pasta, special every day. Romantic? Bottle of Chianti. A corny shtick? Sure. But Lynn's Italian mom was the main cook and she had some kickass recipes, bein' from Naples and all, and Lynn grew up cookin' too. All kinds of seafood too. Jeez, wouldn't it be great if this joint could eventually serve pasta with squid ink and clams. *Arrivederci* baby.

Ralphie, he had an Italian dad and a German mom, but we're talking way back. They came over on that boat to Ellis Island. Ralphie was a Jersey boy through and through.

So now, here he was in in his thirties. For a few years Ralphie had asked himself, *What the hell am I doin' in this place? I'm a*

Boardwalk boy, an Atlantic City guy. Low roller... Sure, but he'd been happy.

What happened was that he and Lynn got hitched. Ralphie had made most of his money hauling stuff in warehouses and driving trucks, but he got a little spare cash here and there from the "Vincento thing," pushing Blu-ray players off the back of vans and such.

So he knew some guys. Lynn, she wanted her own restaurant. And Ralphie had always talked big. "Yeah, babe. It's you and me. Whatcha want? I'm pulling in some cash."

Unfortunately, he'd been having bad luck with the bookies. Sheesh, they made that kind of luck in hell. He'd pulled out soon enough, but here was the beautiful and wonderful Lynn wanting a simple thing. A restaurant! And so Ralphie, not wanting to lose Lynn, had gone to the Vincento for a little cash.

He'd gotten it.

At first the place did okay, but then, geez, the fuckin' Great Recession hit. Folks started buying frozen Walmart pizza, and only the stable restaurants survived.

Not Lynn's Italian Specialties.

So guess who turned up. Why, it was Freddie Monteleone, Freddie from the mob. And guess who didn't have a payment. Couple times like that, a couple of broken fingers, and Ralphie knew it was time to get out.

He had a little on the side and so did Lynn. And he said one evening, holding up his cast, "Baby, we gotta get outta here."

They were on the train the next day. They went this way and that, and they used fake IDs.

They stopped in Colorado for a while, but it was too expensive. In Colorado Springs, they heard about a place in the West that was like the East only with dreadful pizza.

Eugene, Oregon.

Bingo.

When Ralphie and Lynn got to Eugene, Lynn loved it. Ralphie thought it was the strangest place he'd ever been too, but it wasn't as rainy as he'd thought it would be, and shit! The pizza was total crap. Moreover, it was only spring then and flowers were in bloom; people were venturing out and they went to a thing called the Saturday Market. Huddled around a stage and some picnic tables were food carts! There was a pizza cart there. Crap! He let Lynn have a taste.

"Jesus Christ, what is this crust? Cardboard?"

"They say the cheese is *organic*. So what is imported mozzarella from Italy, huh? *In*organic?"

Lynn laughed. They both liked *Star Trek*.

They stayed a week at a cheap hotel on 99. Bought a good car at a good price. Found a cheap apartment. And they still had plenty of their stash left.

Ralphie was impressed. "You know, I hate to say this Lynn, but if I didn't like this place, I was planning on doing some kind of quick con job or somethin', something simple and splittin'. But hell, no way now! I don't want to soil my new nest."

Lynn was happy. She was sad she couldn't contact her family yet, but give that a year or so, she could have them out here. Maybe a new house! Yeah, they had some nice ones back in those South Hills.

So, what he did was, Ralphie bought himself a food cart. The cheap pickup already had a hitch that worked in its rear. They fixed it up. My Mama's Best Pizza they called it. They found a good place to set up for the lunch and dinner crowd, and they got a permit. What they didn't have was a decent oven. That proved easy enough to deal with. Ralphie and Lynn made friends with Peter and Kate over at Tie-Dyed Pies just a block away from them on Monroe (crap pizza, but okay fresh basil). They baked their pies there, then warmed them in a cheap portable oven. They were gonna sell just slices first and then maybe branch out to special customers.

Everyone liked the pizza. Lynn had found an inexpensive wholesale international place and she got decent imported New York and Italian ingredients. They kept it simple. You got your plain cheese, you got your pepperoni, you got your onion and pepper and you got the best, Lynn's own recipe for Italian sausage, which she made at home. All with first-class Romano dry cheese. You wanna Coke? You gotta Coke. Things go better…

Trouble was, only a few people *got* the pizza. There was a joint over by the university that advertised New York Style pizza. Ralphie almost threw up. Too much sauce. Shit cheese. And the crust was fuckin' Bisquick!

But the place gave him an idea.

He added "Real 'Tony Soprano' New Jersey pizza" to the sign.

Business improved. Pretty soon some of the other pizza guys came around.

"Not bad. Where are you from?"

"Philly," said Ralphie.

And hell no, no recipes for no body!

And then Phil Roman started coming.

"Hey, you must like this place," Ralphie said to him on his fifth visit. You buy three slices—always."

The fat guy had shrugged. "I like Lynn. Pizza is like sex. Even when it's bad, it's good."

Ralphie managed to keep a smile on his face. "You like my wife, huh?"

"She's married to you? Wow. Lucky guy."

"Yeah, I think so. What's your name?" They shook hands and got acquainted.

"You know the main problem with this pizza?"

"You gotta a problem with my pizza?" said Lynn, just walking in on the conversation.

"Not *per se*. Pizza is like sex—"

"All right, big guy. Just shut up with that bit around my wife, huh?"

"What I mean is," Phil laughed, "it isn't the best pizza in the world—Chicago-style pizza."

It was then that Ralphie almost lost it. This kind of rudeness, from an asshole, eating his wife's cooking? Lynn was speechless. Ralphie was seeing red.

"This, what is it, Bronx-style? They serve this at the zoo?"

It was at that moment that Ralphie realized first that he'd gained more control than he thought. The red faded and he didn't kill the guy. But also, he knew from that moment that he was gonna take this fool for a ride. Somehow, somewhen, someway.

"Lynn, I think I need a Coke. We gotta tell our new friend here what we're up to. He seems like a businessman."

"I am."

"Have a seat, Phil."

Pretty soon, they started making Phil pizzas to take home. He was really just a fat, lonely guy who liked good food, so Ralphie was glad he hadn't hit him. But he also had money. And Ralphie always needed money.

Ralphie started going to Phil's strip joints. Ralphie started to read old crime paperbacks Phil would sell him. Pretty soon, they had him over for spaghetti and meatballs. Phil had liked that.

It was Lynn who started asking Phil for help with their dream—their own regular pizza joint.

And she also promised something special on the menu, if he helped them. Just for him.

And now! Well, tonight was the night.

And there he was. In his ripped Betty Page t-shirt, his huge Dickie workpants, his huge tennis shoes, and a new haircut which made him look more like Oliver Hardy than ever.

"Something certainly smells good in here," said Phil, walking in.

"I believe that something is cooking in the oven with your name on it."

Lynn pointed up at the big menu above the front counter.

"Phil's Chicago-Style Pizza. Whole Pie. Ask for today's Market Price."

Ralphie smiled. He remembered the day he'd suggested the Chicago pie thing to Lynn.

"Look, this guy has got deep pockets. We're already into him for fifty g's and he's so convinced we're his buddies, we didn't have to sign a contract. Let's give him his Chicago pie."

"That barbarian! That fool. That's not pizza. That's Polish or something. It's like a pizza bowl for pigs."

"Hey look. I know how you feel. I shudder at the thought. What can I say? I hear when Phil goes to one of the all-you-can-eat buffets in town, the manager has to come out and stop him from eating everything. We make him his Chicago pies, he gives us more money for more carts. And maybe a little trip to Vegas."

"Gawwwwwd, yes," drawled Lynn in her best *Joisy* accent. "I could sure use a vacation."

"Yep. Get me to tables with decent odds… these Indian casinos around here are robbers of the old and lame. Yeah… and wait, didn't you once go to see a relative in Chicago? And she worked in a pizza place there. She must have shown you the Chicago style."

"Yeah. Marge. So what if she did? It's easy. You chop stuff up. You put in some cheap pie crust. You put it all in with oregano. You bake it."

"Baby, with your sausage and your tastes… Wouldn't your Chicago pie be great?"

"Yeah. But don't make me eat one."

"Did I say you had to eat one?"

"No."

And so, "Phil's Chicago-Style Pizza" was born (although Lynn insisted on calling the result an "abortion").

So there he was.

"You sit back there, Phil. Whatcha want to drink, eh?"

"Just a great big glass of ice water," he said, bellying toward the back.

"Lynn. We got the pie?"

"Yeah."

"Okay. So you know what we planned, right? I serve it up, then go into the kitchen or whatever. Then you go in and talk to Phil and make your pitch. And whacko. Off we go to Vegas."

"Yeah, okay."

"Baby, you can charm the birds off the trees when there are cats around. Saved my butt more than once around wise guys."

"Yeah. Guess I forget I'm a female sometimes."

"Honey, you know I can't forget that!" He winked and patted her rump. She cursed but smiled.

The huge pie was cooling. Seemed to weigh more than a brick. Ralphie needed both arms to haul it in to Phil.

"And *voila!* Here we go, Phil."

Phil sniffed at it suspiciously. "Something's wrong."

"Well, it ain't UNOS. It's Lynn's own version. All the ingredients you asked for…and Wop cooking skill."

Phil delicately cut himself a huge slice. The gooey mess clumped onto the white china like a dead thing, oozing tomato blood.

Phil cut off a piece. He put it in his mouth, chewed. Something weird clicked in his mouth.

Phil smiled.

"I can't do this," he said. "I try and I try. I can't."

"You like, my friend?"

"I like."

"Good. You enjoy. We'll check on you later."

"Thanks, Ralph. Yeah, this works."

He kissed Lynn. "Baby, what a cook."

"Maybe he likes my spit."

He laughed. "Hell, I do!"

They laughed.

16

It was a bright night, and not stormy at all.

In fact, for the season, it was a pleasantly warm.

What people noted when they came to Eugene from the east was how low the sky seemed. The clouds scraped the buttes, and often hung oppressively in the winter when they rendered everything so dark that folks needed special lighting to spend time under for an hour or so each day to cheer up. It was a city of S.A.D. (Seasonal Affective Disorder) and people who were lured here in the hot and sunny summers, stayed for the gorgeous autumns, and were often totally repelled by the darkness and drizzle and yes, cold, of the winter.

The group that stood outside the Eugene Hotel all had their separate thoughts and feelings about the night, and they kept them to themselves.

Maddy loved the weather. The winter was like a bright promise of spring, with blossoming flowers and trees seeming to go green overnight. Bullfinch, who'd visited before, but was hardly familiar with the seasons, took it all in, storing facts as he always did. He liked to think he could close his eyes and mentally walk down any of the more interesting roads he'd taken over a long life—the key was in the details.

Bill just wanted it all to be over with. Ghosts, nooses, murders. He had been doing his job for a long time, and this—this was not the job. It was something else, and it pissed him off.

"Okay," he said, breaking the silence. "I got permission from the precinct, and I'm here officially." He jingled the keys. "I am armed, but I don't have the dousing rods. Think that's okay?"

Bullfinch smiled, and Maddy rolled her eyes. Neither spoke. "Okay, then. Here we go."

"Before we do," Bullfinch said, "take these. I know it will seem odd, but please humor me. I have an odd hunch they will come in handy..."

He handed each of them a small silver crucifix, dangling from a chain. Bill looked as if he might refuse it, but then, he took it and stuffed it in his pocket, turning back to the door without a word.

The part of the hotel that was supposed to be haunted was upstairs. There was an attic that the people who had offices, stores, and restaurants in the building simply did not visit. It wasn't just odd sounds. People had experienced cold spots and reported strange sensations. If the apparitions and strange occurrences had leaked down into the rest of the building, there would never have been anyone there at all. As it turned out, since the "haunting" had remained isolated to the attic, the hotel had become a popular place. People liked to sit and talk about the "ghosts" from below, because it felt safe. Nothing actually *bad* had ever happened.

There was a central hallway in the western side of the building. This was what Bill had the keys to, along with the attic. There was a basement, but there had been no report of paranormal activity there. No one was really surprised; the ghosts were thought to be ladies of the evening, and most of their customers would have preferred soft beds to cold stone walls.

The three climbed the front steps and stood while Bill worked the old lock and pocketed the keys. The door opened easily enough. Well oiled. Clean and quick.

Bill reached in, fumbled for the switch, and flipped on the lights. A line of old-fashioned hanging lamps lit a long corridor. Along the walls to either side were office doors with marked signs on frosted glass.

"My friend, Phillip, said that he used to have a book store right here," said Bullfinch, tapping a window marked WILLAMETTE

ANTIQUES. "Never did especially well, but he enjoyed it. Then came the Internet, and the need to spend so much on overhead disappeared."

"Oh, right. I think I remember that," said Maddy. "That guy. He's kind of large and obnoxious?"

"That he is. He's actually a pretty good man, but he doesn't want anyone to know it—so he works at pushing people away."

"He's good at it," Maddy said.

They had reached the second corridor.

The doors they passed were mostly law offices. Shyster, Shyster, & Shyster, Accident & Injury; Shyster and Shyster and Shyloc, tax lawyers. Shyster, Shyser, Shyster, & Brown, Family Law and Criminal Defense.

Maddy didn't like lawyers.

Bill was no fan.

Young men and women graduated from the local law school and they liked the town, so they stayed. Result? A lot of lean and hungry lawyers snarling and biting over whatever cases they could get, not making the money they thought they deserved, but unwilling to move on to "greener pastures" to get it.

"Funny. These lawyers don't get ghost seepage from upstairs," Maddy said.

"You'd think they would, being lawyers and all," said Bill.

"It's actually not uncommon for spirits to remain centralized in one part of a building," Bullfinch said.

Bill stopped abruptly in front of a less auspicious door with no glass window.

"This is the place," he said.

The door was painted a very plain brown. There was a sign outside that said, ATTIC - NO ENTRY.

Bill flipped through the keys on the ring. "It also leads to the roof," he said. "Let's get this over with."

17

Sky had insisted that Hildy, who was watching him while his mom was off with Bullfinch and Bill, take him back to visit with Adam Even. He'd gathered up an armful of VHS tapes and DVD cases and tucked them into an old backpack.

"He said he'd sign them," Sky said. "And he doesn't have copies of some of them. He said he'd like to meet you too—but mom wasn't too happy. I think, if she remembers, she wants to talk to you about Mr. Even's movies..."

"I just bet she does," Hildy said, eyeing the pile. "It's really him, huh? Right here in Eugene. It's just too weird.

"It's him. It was when I mentioned 'Big Balls' that mom started getting weird.

Hildy shook her head. "I'd better get more beer while we're out," she said. "I can hear that lecture winding up now. Let's get on the road and get this over with."

"We have to pick up Natosha on the way," Sky said. "I promised her if we went back she could come."

Hildy stared at him, started to ask something, then let it go with a nod.

"I'm going to guess she didn't mention 'Big Balls' to her parents..."

Skylar grinned. "I'm sure that she didn't. I think she liked Mr. Even though. He's very funny..."

"So you've said. We'll need to get there as quick as we can—I don't want to be keeping your friend out too late, and it's already starting to get dark."

The four of them were seated in Adam Even's living room, having pushed enough things aside to free up horizontal space. Skylar and Natosha were on the couch, Even was in an old recliner, and Hildy had perched herself near the front edge of an upholstered chair full of books.

Hildy laughed. She had a wonderful laugh, Hildy did. Rich and strong and full of genuine mirth.

"I can't believe how funny this movie is," she said. "*Boobs from Outer Space* with Cameron Mitchell and Byron James! And a guest appearance by none other than Mrs. Gene Simmons herself, Shannon Tweed. And you were in a hot tub with those huge bobbing breasts. Hubba hubba!"

"Oh yeah," said Adam Even. "That was pleasant. And a very nice lady, too. I can't believe you've brought me a copy of this. I didn't have it. I'm so touched!"

"That you definitely are," Hildy said.

"Speaking of hot tubs," said Sky. "We also have *Hollywood Hot Tubs*.

"Thanks, but I have that one," Even said, leaning back in his chair.

"Hey. You knew John Belushi, didn't you?" Sky asked.

"I did. He and Robin Williams and I used to hang out sometimes. I'm not dropping names here either. Let me show you something."

Adam Even got up, brushed some stray popcorn from his sweatpants, and rushed off into another room.

"He seems excited about something," said Hildy.

"Yes. I think we have made a friend. A good friend."

"Looks like he's got quite the video library, too."

"And a lot of stories," said Sky.

"I don't know," said Natosha, who had remained oddly silent through the entire visit to that point. "Now that it's night, I feel kinda spooked here."

She looked up at the ceiling, shuddering.

"Your mother mentioned some kind of cat noises up there,"

Hildy said. "I haven't heard anything…"

"Don't hear any now." Skylar shrugged.

"Yes. But I kind of feel something weird. Know what I mean?" Natosha frowned.

Hildy laughed. "Haven't a clue. I'm mercilessly unattached to the morbid and have given up anxiety a very long time ago."

"Well, I sure feel something. You, Sky?"

"Yes. And I do smell cats. Not as bad as at your house, Hildy, but still…"

They were interrupted as Adam Even re-entered the room. He was grinning from ear to ear. He held a long something, robed in richly textured black cloth. A kind of string hung from one side, or a knotted cord.

"*Voila!*" said Adam Even. "A most remarkable item indeed."

"Pray tell, sir," said Hildy. "What is it?"

"Ah ha! Back in the early Eighties, right after John had finished his work with *Saturday Night Live* and pretty much lived in L.A. full time, there was one week where he made a *lot* of money. So he bought presents for all his friends and gave them to us at a special party. And this was mine!"

Adam Even undraped the horizontal object.

"It's a sword!" said Sky.

"It's not just any sword…" said Adam Even. "It's a sword celebrating his series of sketches on *SNL!*"

"Hai!" said Adam Even, grinning.

The sword was a beautiful thing indeed, a long sheath, topped with a beautiful carved handle, black, black and black.

"A very nice sword indeed!" said Sky.

Adam Even said, "Oh, not just any sword!" He stepped back and pulled it out. It sang as he slipped it from the sheath, a whisper song of cherry blossoms and silent snow in cedars.

"It's a samurai sword!" said Natosha, finally seeming interested. "Cool!"

"And what a gift! From the samurai guy himself!" said Hildy.

"What?" Natosha asked, turning toward Hildy.

"Oh, yes. I should show you my *Best of John Belushi on Saturday Night Live* DVD," Sky said. "He was Samurai this, and Samurai that. Samurai Donut Maker, Samurai Shoe Salesman. Always deadpan in full getup and this awesome black wig. And he'd end up hacking something up with his sword and shouting 'Hai!'"

"Oh yes. Like those wonderful Zatoichi movies you showed me. And *Seven Samurai*," Sky said.

"Awesome movie!" said Natosha.

Adam Even gazed at the shiny blade. Light reflected from it into his eyes, and they didn't seem so dark anymore, but instead a soft velvet hazel. "And look. John had it engraved for us. You don't want to get too close to the blade. It's sharp as a razor. I'll just read it, shall I?"

"Sure!" said Hildy.

"'To Adam. A wizard, a true star.'"

He smiled.

"John knew I was a Todd Rundgren fan, you see. That's the name of a Todd Rundgren album."

Carefully, he reinserted the blade in its sheath.

He placed it carefully in its cloth and put it down by his chair. He took up his popcorn and said, "Okay. Where were we?"

A few more bouncing naked breasts later, there began a peculiar screeching shaking. It sounded vaguely like a train. The noise rose, sudden and loud. It shivered through the house and set all their hair on end. It sounded like a cat in heat. No… two cats mating. No… three cats, four having a screeching, painful orgy.

The house started to shake. Adam Even looked out the window.

"Damned freight trains! That's the problem with this place. And the cats hate 'em!"

The rumbling continued, and then there was a sudden smashing, like vases breaking, followed by what sounded like the coarse death rattle of desert wind, pushing some ancient opening.

The rumble continued for a moment, but then there was silence.

Adam Even took no notice.

He took a handful of popcorn and stuffed it in his mouth.

The others exchanged startled glances. Natosha moved closer to Skylar on the couch. As the rumble of the train faded, they returned their attention to Adam's old television.

On screen, Adam Even drove off with Heather Thomas in a Volkswagen bug. Trailing them were old boots and shreds of confetti.

On the back of the Volkswagen bug was a sign that read, *Just Married and About to Fuck Our Brains Out.*

Hildy glanced at Skylar, and Natosha, wishing she'd remembered that was how this one ended before it had passed across the screen, and wondering how much crap she'd have to take if either of them ever mentioned it.

A cheap *The End* sign showed, followed by a crawl of credits to the majestic sound of a third-rate hair metal band.

They all applauded.

Adam Even sat transfixed until the very last credit rolled, and then the tape stopped.

He shook his head.

He looked different.

There was a tear in his eye.

He wiped it away. "Oh. Pardon me. That Heather. She sure could… uhmm… kiss."

"Jesus. You got it on with Heather Locklear?" said Natosha.

"No. No. Heather Thomas. Much better looking, I always said. She was in *The Fall Guy* with Lee Majors."

"*The Six Million Dollar Man!*" said Hildy.

"Guys, I'm totally at sea here. That woman was pretty, though. Don't you think so, Sky?" Nakota said. She watched his expression, clearly interested in what he thought. Skylar didn't notice. He answered with his usual detached distance.

"She does conform with the Eighties' sense of beauty, including that remarkable hair!"

Hildy shook her head. Time to take charge of this before it

got out of hand. "Well, that was super," she said, "but the kids are up late, and I think maybe it's time to go."

"Oh sure, sure," Adam said. "Of course. Thanks for bringing that tape over. I'm popping it out for you now. Don't want you not to come back. Maybe you got other films I don't even remember. Early Eighties I did a hell of a lot of cocaine and drank like a fish. I toured and did a bunch of movies. Most of the money went to my dishonest manager. So yeah, I'd like to see more. But hey... there's one more thing I want to show you. Can you hold your horses for like half a minute?

"Uhm, sure. I guess."

"Thanks. Thanks so much."

Adam Even got up, brushed the popcorn crumbs off his lap, and hurried off into that other room from where he'd brought the John Belushi samurai sword.

Hildy looked at her watch. "Well, it's not all that late, I guess."

Natosha looked troubled, squinting her dark mascaraed eyes.

"I don't know," she said. "Something tells me it's later than we think."

It took a few minutes, but when Adam Even returned, he did have something in his hands.

"Now I'm hoping you guys still all have cassette tape players," he said.

They all did.

"Good. If not, I think I've got a couple Goodwill six-buck specials. But you do!"

"They're cassettes?" said Skylar.

"What's on them?" asked Natosha.

"Me! Here, one for each of you."

Adam Even handed them out one by one.

Hildy looked at hers. It was just a picture of the much younger Adam Even standing by a stool, leaning into a mike on a proscenium, with a spotlight limning him like some full body halo.

"It's still got cellophane on it!" said Hildy.

"Yep. No corrosion of tape. This is one of only a thousand

copies I had done of me at the Troubadour in L.A. June seventh, nineteen eighty-one. Robin Williams was in the audience. So were John Belushi, Danny Aykroyd, and lots of other comedians. Probably the best stand-up show I ever did."

"Wow!" said Sky.

"Yep. You know what Steve Martin says about stand up. It's easy to be great once in a while, but it's hard to always be good. I was never always good—but this time, I was great. And yeah, I think Steve was there, too."

"Can't wait to hear it."

"Yes, folks. At that show…this comedian killed."

"Would you sign it?" asked Skylar.

"Sure, Sky. Gonna have to rip off the cellophane. Might lose value…especially if I sign it," said Adam Even.

They all wanted their gifts signed.

"Sure. Just let me go back to my study. I got a Flair there that should work."

He was back in just a moment, brandishing the marker with a grin.

"There you go," said Adam Even. He finished signing the last of the cassette tapes, Skylar's, managing to get a long personalization into it. "Thanks guys. This all means a lot to me and…"

Suddenly, there was a crash. This time the sound was louder. It came from a room upstairs. It sounded like cats in heat, whirling, chasing each other's tails.

"Damned things," said Adam Even. "You know they might just need the company of some nice people." He smiled charmingly and ingratiatingly. "I know they sound terrible, but they are all quite beautiful. Would you like to go up with me and see them?"

"Yes," said Skylar.

18

The door creaked open. It creaked and squeaked, making a terrible old-fashioned special horror movie sound effect as it opened.

Maddy gasped.

Bill Edmonds stepped back, startled at the sudden sound.

Even the usually imperturbable Bullfinch raised his eyebrows and felt his pulse quicken.

"Looks like nobody oils these hinges," Bill said. The keys jingled some more as he took them out of the lock, reached in and fumbled for the light switch.

"Shit." He pulled out his flashlight, clicked it on, and shone it to the sides.

"There it is," said Edmonds.

The steps were old, with faded gray carpet, worn and thin over the cracked wood. The wallpaper to either side was peeling. Above, where a naked bulb hung in a fixture, dust motes danced in the dim light, like disturbed sprites. Their footsteps echoed up the stairs, and Bill's light danced up into the extreme shadows. As they reached the top, the first thing they noticed was the change in temperature.

It was cold. The kind of English Thames-side chill that bites through coats on bat wings of fog.

"Good heavens," breathed Bullfinch. "A cold spot. Already?"

"Cold spot?" said Maddy.

"Yes. Haunted houses often have areas where the temperatures dive for no apparently natural reason."

"Hence, *super*natural," Bill said cynically. He shivered despite himself and Maddy could tell he wasn't happy about being there, or the way things were going.

"The 'tools of the trade' on television are, for the most part, toys. They scan radio frequencies for random sounds, check for electromagnetic fields, but rarely find anything that wouldn't be there wherever you looked. I believe we're going to have to be a little more creative if we want real results," said Bullfinch. He took a deep breath of the frigid air. "Let's have a look upstairs then, shall we?"

He stepped forward and flashed what he called his "torch" around. He needed it. The light from the dangling bulb was dim and seemed to soak into the shadows before it reached the floor. Edmonds was happy he'd brought his own light and that he'd insisted Maddy do the same.

"So, what are we looking for?" Bill asked

The beams of their lights cut through the shadows in odd patterns. What they revealed was this:

Sheets.

Well, they seemed like sheets, anyway. Drop cloths? Covers? In any case, they were draped over mounds great and small that were spread out over a large expanse of floor. Some parts of that floor were covered by old rugs. Other parts were bare. The bare parts showed ancient stained wood littered with the ragged ends of nails sticking up like they'd been pounded into a coffin that had been pried open.

"Let's have a look. I think the temperature drop is more severe over here."

Bullfinch walked over to a dusty sheet covering a small mound. He peeled it back. They stared. Beneath it, there were three chests.

"This," Bullfinch said with satisfaction, "is what we are looking for. What do you suppose we're going to find in these, detective?"

"Spooks?"

"Far too easy. Maddy?"

"Nooses."

"That would be my guess. I'd also wager they will be identical to those used in the recent 'suicides'. Detective, would you do the honors?"

Bill stepped forward and examined the chest closest to them. He bent and gripped the lid with both hands. There was no lock; the chest opened easily. He lifted the lid. Inside was what looked like piles and piles of curtains, along with rings. Bullfinch bent over, rummaged through it for a moment.

"Ah, well. Nothing much here," he said at last.

The second trunk was filled with old china.

"Well then," Bullfinch said. "Shall I give the last one a look?"

"Be my guest, good sir," said Maddy curtseying. Bill turned away to prevent the others noticing his smile. Bullfinch raised an eyebrow, and then turned his attention to the final chest.

"That's different," he said. "This one appears to be locked." He turned and showed them a small, ornate padlock dangling from a hasp.

Bill pulled out a wire cutter, and using both hands, made short work of the lock.

"Thought this little baby might come in handy."

"Would you care to do the honors, Maddy?"

Maddy looked around. In the far corner, there was a rocking chair, uncovered, standing by a piano, which was also uncovered. Had she heard a tinkle of keys? Imagination, surely. But still…

"There's so much stuff up here."

"I'm thinking there's more than one of what we're looking for here," said Bullfinch. "And the chests are similar to those that others have described—they feel like the right place to look first."

Maddy shrugged. She opened the chest. The lid flipped up silently, as though the hinges had been oiled recently.

Bill directed the beam of his flashlight into the interior. What it illuminated was a bundle of neatly pressed linens. Napkins, tablecloths, and such. Old stuff, hotel stuff. It all smelled of mothballs.

Bullfinch knelt by the chest and fingered the linen thoughtfully. He dug deeper.

His hand slipped beneath the linens, met coarse hemp, and he grew very still. Then, with a small flourish, he pulled the noose free of its hiding place and held it up for the other to see.

It swung and dangled. The longer part of the old rope was still in the chest. He'd pulled it out like a cobra's head from a basket in some Indian bazaar.

"Jesus," said Edmonds. "You were right. A noose."

"And just like the others!" said Maddy.

"Exactly like the others," Bullfinch corrected. "To the last detail."

He rose slowly and hauled the remainder of the rope free of the chest.

"All of the others were found in chests," Maddy said. "In basements, and in… attics."

"Maddy. When did the first member of the Noose Club discover his deadly antique," Bullfinch asked. "Do you know?"

"Not precisely," she said. "About nine years ago."

"Recently, then. Not a local legend, or something that's been dragging on for decades. If you remember these nooses were supposed to be from back in the late nineteenth century, and presumably, if we go with the vengeful ghost theory, the result of the Claude Blanchford hanging."

"You sound as though you aren't buying it," said Maddy.

"Never believed it for a moment. Good Lord, people were hung all the time in the American West. It was a carryover from being a popular sport in England. I could tell you stories…" He sighed. "But I won't. The point is, if that sort of thing could cause an epidemic of haunted suicides like we are experiencing, they would be commonplace. There was nothing particularly remarkable about that hanging."

"So," Maddy said, "you're saying that all of these were planted. But not by ghosts?"

"Possibly," Bullfinch said. "It is also possible that I simply need to expand my appreciation and understanding of what spirits are capable of. I mean, what we are standing in is a classic, cold spot. That is typical of nearly all hauntings, and would seem to indicate that is what we are up against. But…"

"Tell me about it," said Maddy. "I've got goosebumps on my goosebumps. Does that make them ghost bumps?"

"Ha ha ha," Bill said.

Bullfinch smiled thinly. "In any case, we have what I was looking for. But as long as we are here, let's peer about, shall we? If the noose is here, maybe we can find some indication of how it came to be here—who, or what, planted it."

They all turned, scanning the remainder of the attic. It was a very big space with deep shadows. Bullfinch draped the noose and rope over his shoulder as they slowly walked forward, Edmonds' beam piercing the dimness. Off to the north part of the attic, there were no cold spots. In fact, things got a bit humid and musty.

"Jesus, what a change," said Edmonds. "I'm not sure I like it."

"Oh, but you should," said Bullfinch. "Look around us. In this section, the attic is just as it was described. It's piled high with things that no one wants, things that have been more or less forgotten. It's my estimation that the grade and quality of antiques in Oregon—especially a more marginal area like Eugene—are not worth so much. Hence all of this remains in place, not valuable enough for someone to cross that other area closer to the door to haul it out and try to sell it."

"Yes. People don't want to come up here," said Maddy.

"Now look up there. Now that's interesting. Bill, were you informed of that?"

He pointed.

What he pointed at was a set of steps leading up to the darker shadows by the ceiling.

"Yeah," Bill said. "That would be the way up to the roof. That's required by safety regulations."

"That makes sense," Bullfinch said, "but it's coated in dust. Doesn't anyone use it? Inspections?"

"Not really. There are fire escapes on the side of the building. I

think if anyone has to go up to the roof, they use those. It avoids...
this." Bill waved a hand to indicate the space between the three
of them and the doorway through which they'd entered.

"Well, I think we'd better have a look," Bullfinch said. "We
found the noose, but there has to be more to it, and the rest of the
attic seems rather benign."

"Suits me," Bill said. "At least the air out there should be
fresh."

"Do we have to?" said Maddy. "I don't need more goosebumps on my goosebumps. Haven't you already proved that
someone has been placing these nooses around town, and that
it's not something supernatural?"

"I never said anything of the sort," said Bullfinch. "I said I
did not believe that the nooses were related to the historic hanging. But," he brought a hand to his forehead and fell silent for a
second, "please... I feel something...distinctly odd."

He turned toward the stairway leading upward, his eyes suddenly very bright. It was almost as if he'd scented something,
or heard something of vast importance. He took a step, then
another, half reluctantly, then suddenly hurried to the steps. He
found himself unusually winded. Something was clearly bother-
ing him. He stopped at the base of the stairs, as if he had to catch
his breath. Bill's light showed a fine sheen of sweat formed on his
brow.

Then his back arched, as if an electric shock had run through
him, and he nearly fell backward from the impact of it.

In his mind, he heard a voice. A woman's voice, calling out
to him. He knew the words were directed at him, but knew at
the same time that something was wrong... something about the
names...

"Thomas. Please. I'm up here..." He shook his head again,
but the voice continued. "Please, I need you!"

It was her!

Oh good Lord. But how could it be? That had been years ago.
So many, many years.

Bullfinch stood frozen, holding onto the wooden railing of the stairs as though to support himself.

"Charity," he whispered. "Charity Marchcliff."

"Thomas. Oh please, you have to help me. I'm up here. I'm up here! Please, darling. it's been so, so long, but now you're here!"

Hesitantly at first, and then more quickly, Bullfinch mounted the stairs and started up toward the roof.

"Hey, wait," said Edmonds. "That thing's got to be locked. You want to go up to the roof? Fine. But come back down and let me go up and open it for you, okay?"

Bullfinch ignored him. All he could hear was Charity, and all he could think of was the memory of her sweet embrace— and the darkness, the chasm that had parted them for years. He smelled her now, the sweet floral smell, the lace and chamomile soap scent that floated around her like a cloud. Her glorious auburn hair, floating in an autumn sunset.

"Bullfinch! What the fuck?"

Bullfinch reached the top of the stairs. The trap door was concave, made of some strong, opaque plastic. Bullfinch pushed hard—and it opened for him, like the doorway to Aladdin's cave.

The cool of night swam in. He scampered up, more agile than his years would suggest was possible.

"Hey, wait for us!" Maddy called from below. "What's wrong with you?"

It was a flat roof, with raised pipes, air conditioning and heating units, and vents sprinkled across a wide, open space. Steam issued from an opening. A tool shed stood to the right. In the distance, a train wailed its sad song to the darkness.

Breathing hard, Bullfinch spun slowly, surveying the area.

A three-quarter moon hung over the quiet city, just lifting up from beside Spencer's Butte to the south. Stars hung in the sky, as though holding up a few puppet cumulus clouds by threads. It smelled of tar and stone.

And then he saw her.

"Charity!" he called out.

She stood down by the edge. There was a vent or a pipe very close to her. Steam rose from it, circling her and rising to form. Right by there seemed to be some sort of chimney pot. Steam rose to form a halo around her head. She wore Edwardian clothes that were so charming. That shawl... the flowing dress... Her bright eyes seemed to shine—as bright as the stars overhead.

"Thomas," she said. "My foot is caught? See? If you could help me, we could be together again."

He crossed the roof slowly, making it about halfway to where she waited, and then he caught himself.

What was he thinking? Charity was dead, long dead. And this woman seemed so solid, no ghost at all. And... Thomas? Was he...

He stopped and started to turn away.

"Oh no you don't, you motherfucker!"

The shock of the language spun him back around. The form of his old love had been transformed from beautiful young girl to a creature. A demon's face appeared. Hands stretched out, morphing to claws. With inhuman speed, the thing launched itself at him, eyes blazing.

"Bastard!" it screamed. "You're gonna get yours."

Strong arms clutched his body. The fetid stench of dead flesh enveloped him. He gagged and tried to struggle, but felt helpless in the thing's grasp.

He was dragged toward the edge of the building, feet slipping and sliding on the rough surface of the roof.

"Remember your Dickens, old man? Remember *Oliver Twist*?" In another blur, the noose he'd been carrying since it was unearthed in the attic below was suddenly slipped over his head. "Well, Mr. Myth, give my regards to Bill Sykes."

And then, Bulfinch saw it.

Surrounded in a cape of squamous night, it flowed and drifted in bands of thorns and chains. Razor blades and Sweeny Todd swirled, shrieking, though the din. Snarling faces and images he could not bring into focus filled his vision.

With a huge lurching shove, Bullfinch was pushed toward the edge of the building.

The creature writhed. It writhed like a nest of snakes. It hissed and roared. Its sharp teeth gnashed. And it laughed.

Bullfinch was hurled backward. He was caught by the raised brick border just below the buttocks, but the force of the shove carried his head and torso over the edge and tilted him back over thin air.

Gasping, he tilted, reaching around and twisting down. The torque spun him around like an athlete doing a maneuver on a gymnastic horse. He clamped his legs, cried out, felt his grip slip… and he went over. With a surge of adrenalin and fear, he gripped the edge with his left hand, and held.

The thing laughed, holding the rope. Hissed and laughed like a chuckling furnace.

Bullfinch scraped and scrabbled on the edge, boots digging at the brick as he slipped a bit, then tightened his grip and held. He managed to get his right hand onto the ledge as well, clinging with all his strength and thankful for long hours in the mountains.

"No!" he cried.

"Oh yessssss!" said the thing. Still snarling and chuckling, it tied the rope around a ventilator pot and seemed to float slowly toward its quarry. "Yesss!"

Bullfinch gripped hard with his strongest hand and arm, his right. With his left, he reached into the left pocket of his jacket. He pulled out a vial.

"The noose is too looooosssssse!" hissed the creature. "Letsssss tighennnnn…"

Bullfinch began to chant in a strong, measured tone. The words were Latin.

He waited. He spoke clearly, forcing his voice to remain steady…

And then he tossed the vial.

It flew up and over, like a sparkling grenade. Made of wafer-thin glass, it smashed on contact with the being leering down at him, dissolving into amorphous clouds and splashing up, down, and into the thing. It was a direct hit, and the creature screamed.

"Son of a bitch!" cried a voice from behind the struggle.

What Captain Bill Edmonds saw when he pulled himself up through the entrance to the roof shook the very roots of the universe as he knew it. It wasn't a man, or a woman. It seemed to be a ball of whirling energy. Except, that wasn't it, not exactly. He saw what looked like clouds, or mist, crackling with lightning. No, that wasn't it, there were claws and snapping jaws and maws filled with gnashing teeth and crushed bones.

Whatever it was had a vaguely human shape, and it was headed for the edge of the building.

But where the hell was Bullfinch for God's sake...

And he saw the hands, gripping the edge of the roof. Human hands.

The thing, creature, whatever-it-was, flashed, like someone had shot it with brilliant white light. It staggered for a moment. The swirl of mist shrunk in on itself, its crazy, surreal motion stilled, and then it solidified.

What was left was a squat, twisted, hunchbacked horror.

"Son of a bitch!" Bill yelled.

He wasn't much good at a desk job. He had been a Marine, and when he was a Marine his hunting and gun background had stood him well. In the police academy he had done so well at weapons that he'd been recommended to the department down in Los Angeles, where he'd spent several years on a S.W.A.T. team. Now he was stuck at a desk job, but he still went out to the firing range.

He'd brought a brand-new service pistol. Smith & Wesson, .45 caliber. It snapped out of the holster in two quick movements. One more and the safety was off.

He read no Miranda rights.

The first bullet struck the thing square in its back. A gout of some kind of wet, sticky fluid splatted out, almost in slow motion. Not flesh. Something else. Solid first, but then, abruptly amorphous, anamorphous—and then misting up and disappearing into the night.

The thing wailed. It spun around, then moved so fast, it was a blur. He got off one more shot but it was good one. It struck dead center in the thing's chest, splattering more of it to either side, but it barely slowed. It came at him jaws wide and talon-like claws extended.

Bullfinch struggled to get his hand up higher, and to get purchase with his feet. He'd heard the gunshots and the shrieks. He knew he could not hang there much longer. He had to move. He had to keep his grip.

But his fingers were going numb… and he was slipping.

Maddy heard the horrible noises above. She'd hung back to let Bill check out the situation; what she heard didn't sound good. Then the shots rang out and her training kicked in. She hadn't brought a gun, why would she? This wasn't a manhunt—it was just supposed to be a look at the Ghost Hotel.

She launched herself up the last few steps and onto the roof. A few yards away she saw the thing falling on Bill. She couldn't focus on it—it shifted and flickered. Whatever it was, it wasn't human. Without giving it much thought, she pulled out the silver crucifix Bullfinch had entrusted with her, and she held out the vial.

It was an even bigger vial than the one that Bullfinch had thrown. She hurled it first, and then stepped forward, brandishing the crucifix.

Bullfinch clung with the last of his strength. He looked down. His eyes had adjusted to the darkness. He found what he might be looking for.

He managed to start a swing.

He managed to get it started, but it cost him his grip.

The noose was still around his neck; the other end of the rope was tied to the fixture.

Bullfinch fell.

The thing slashed out with a claw and caught Bill a glancing blow. He was quick, though, and stepped back out of danger. He kept his eyes on the thing, ready for the next attack, but it never came. There was flash of glittering light, the tinkle of breaking glass, and the thing was engulfed in blue, flickering light a second time. It lifted its mottled, misshapen head, staggered back, and held out its arms as though picking out a cape from the surrounding darkness. There was one streaky blur and it was gone.

"Bill!"

"I'm fine," gasped Edmonds. "Bullfinch. Hanging on the edge!"

"Oh, Jesus," said Maddy.

They ran down to the edge of the building. Bullfinch was gone.

"Bullfinch!" cried Maddy.

"The rope! Cut the rope! Cut the rope!"

It was Bullfinch's voice.

Maddy peered over the edge. Angled her head. There, struggling, just below, was Geoffrey Bullfinch dangling from a pigeon-spotted ledge. His eyes were wide, and the noose was cinched around his neck.

"The rope! The rope!"

"Oh my God!" said Edmonds.

"Hold on! Hold on!"

But Bullfinch could not hold on. He fingers gave out once again and he tumbled, noose tight around his neck, the slack leaving the rope as it slithered out toward its full length.

Bill swung around and raised his gun.

Part Two

As wicked dew as e'er my mother brush'd
With raven's feather from unwholesome fen
Drop on you both! a south-west blow on ye
And blister you all o'er!

—William Shakespeare,
The Tempest

Bright wings, soft songs; a rare and curious place:
I'd wept, I'd prayed. Then, there! No. Here! God's grace.

—Edward Johnson,
Hymns of Desire

19

At 8 PM in Eugene, Oregon, Phil Roman the bookman sat in his favorite chair at Jiggles, arms folded over his immense abdomen, watching a new girl dance.

Well, maybe dancing wasn't quite the right word. She was swinging around the metal pole, and doing a rather good job of it. She was new, probably from out of town. If she'd danced at the other clubs in town, Phil would know. He went to them all regularly.

He'd asked her about all that when she came around and asked if he wanted a ten-dollar dance. Phil had been prepared, and he had a ten spot out, rolled and held prominently erect.

He sat still, enjoyed the show, and kept his expression molded to its usual state of smugness. Ah yes, life was good.

After his dance (her name was Star and she was from Seattle, headed for Vegas), Ralphie came in.

Phil couldn't help but smile.

"He's alive!" he said.

"You bet, fella," said Ralphie, slapping his good buddy on his back. "Okay if I park this Italian tush for a while?"

"Long as it's not in my face. Your wife? I guess that wouldn't be a problem." Heh heh heh. He laughed his hearty laugh.

Ralphie cringed, but kept a stiff smile.

"Okay. So, you got my book?"

"Yes, indeed."

"What is it this time?"

"*The Girl with the Long Green Heart* by Lawrence Block. Great crime novel."

"Okay. I liked that Donald Westlake you gave me last week."

"Richard Stark. Yep. That Parker novel. *The Hunter*, renamed *Point Blank* for the film. Made into a movie at least twice, best one with Lee Marvin."

"So you say. Tough guy, Parker."

"Yep. Hardboiled."

"I got your pie outside in the car. Hot from the oven."

"Mmmm," said Phil.

"So Lynn and I are headed off to Vegas next week. She mentioned you might want to let us borrow a bit of money for a table. I lose, you get it all back. I win, you get some vigorish."

Phil nodded. "Sure. And we were talking about maybe doing another of your restaurants. Up in Salem. No good pizza there either. Take it from me."

Ralphie grinned and held his hands out. "I'm going to Vegas for fun, yeah, but I'm figuring on bankrolling lots of that from winnings."

"If you're doing your books right, I'm sure you can also get a business loan from a bank. Takes a while."

"We're in no hurry," he smiled the Great American Snake-oil Smile. "So, you got your checkbook, Phil?"

"I don't carry a checkbook. Barely have one anymore. As you know, I like cash."

"Oh. Hmm, like I'm gonna turn down cash?"

"When are you leaving?"

"This weekend," said Ralphie.

"Plenty of time," said Phil. "You know where I live. Come on over in a couple days. That's when the timer on the vault allows me to open it."

Ralphie's face went blank on that.

"Uh, yeah. Right. So… you got a lot of …ah…value in that house," Ralphie said finally.

Phil rolled his eyes. "I'll say. Been working at it for years. That's why I'm retired now and just sell books and pulps and comics."

"You don't say. We got lots of dough in our restaurant. And you got lots of dough at your house."

Phil barked a laugh at that. "Yeah. Yeah, you might say that."

"Okay. Thanks. So, I'll see you in a couple days or so." He got up and waggled the book. "Thanks for *The Girl with the Long Green Heart*!"

"You don't want to stick around for a dance?"

"You payin'?"

"Yep. To buy me one!" said Phil. "Heh heh."

"Fuck you, buddy!" Ralphie grinned. "I got my own action at home."

"I'll say!"

They both laughed.

"And take it from me, no hurry to get home. Those Chicago pies are just as good fresh or reheated."

"Who says I'm taking it home? Got a clean fork in my car."

"Well, wear a bib, Phil. Ciao."

20

Maddy stared. She faced a door—it was Adam Even's door—but she had the vague notion that something was wrong, that the door was wrong, or out of place. She knocked.

She remembered knocking on it once before, but it had been different. This time she had a gun. And a vial of holy water.

She still felt a bit dizzy—the world seemed to tilt, as if it were slowly turning upside down. She blinked, and slammed her hands down on the ledge at the roof's edge, halting her forward progress. She stared over that edge and saw Bullfinch, lying on the ground below. He wasn't moving.

At first she could hear nothing. There was a great rushing, and she nearly keeled over from sudden vertigo. She remembered slowly. Bullfinch's voice. The rope, and the noose... and...

BLAM!

The report from Bill's gun blasting right by her ear had temporarily deafened her. Thank God he was such a good shot! The thick bullet had snapped the rope instantly, and it had gone right over the side, streaming down behind Bullfinch like a long, lost worm, flopping onto his still body. Thankfully, she had not been able to hear the sound of his scream—or the impact of his body striking the ground.

Her vision swam again, and again she knocked on Adam Even's door. Then she rang the doorbell.

The sounds echoed inside her skull, but there was something... what was it? Something bad. Something dangerous she could not quite lay a finger on.

What was it?

The door echoed hollowly at the strike of her knuckles—as if the place was empty, like a giant, hollow drum. She sensed others, knew she had to act...but then...

Bill grabbed her roughly around the waist and yanked her back from the edge of the roof. She shook her head. She knew where she was, knew she could not have knocked on that door, but still... What the hell? Was she becoming psychic, or was someone—or some thing—calling out to her mind?

As soon as she was safe, Bill had slipped his gun back in his holster, pulled out his cell phone and called 911. Maddy pulled her iPhone from her pocket and dialed Hildy's mobile. When Hildy answered, she didn't hesitate. She screamed into the receiver, "Get them out of there! Get the kids out of there now!"

The phone fell from her hand, which felt numb, and clattered on the hard tar surface of the roof. Bill had finished his own call and grabbed her, holding her upright.

"Okay, calm down, calm down," he said. "We've got to get down to Bullfinch."

She looked at him, seeing him clearly for the first time. His shirt, his face, hands, and arms were covered in something dark and liquid. It was too dark to tell for sure what it was, but her heart leapt.

"But you... Blood..."

"Scratches. Just scratches, and most of this is from that—thing. I don't know what you did back there, but you saved my butt."

He had turned and was dragging her toward the door and the stairs leading down. In the distance they could hear the wail of approaching sirens.

Maddy dragged her feet for a moment and grabbed his arm. "Wait... wait, Bill, that thing... what the hell was that?"

"How in hell should I know? I can tell you it wasn't some punk hanging out with a bunch of good special effects. Whatever it was, it was as real as you and I. Still, if that was a ghost, it was like no ghost I've ever heard of." He tugged on her again and started to run. "Come on."

They got down to Bullfinch before the paramedics arrived. Bill knelt down and checked his vitals. He was alive, and though there was a cut on his scalp that was bleeding profusely, he was breathing normally. The odd angles of his limbs spoke of broken bones. Bill did his best to staunch the flow of blood and did what he could to make Bullfinch more comfortable.

"Thank God it wasn't that long a fall." He glanced up. There was a partially torn awning about ten feet overhead. The front support was bent down in the middle. "He must have hit that and bounced... but it partially broke his fall."

"Thank God that noose didn't snap his neck," Maddy said.

Bill glanced down and saw the offending loop of rope still wrapped around Bullfinch's neck. "Yeah. Let's get that thing off of him. There's more than enough to explain here."

Bill managed to loosen the noose and stashed it in his car without being noticed as the ambulance screeched up to the curve, and he and Maddy backed off to let the paramedics take charge. They put Bullfinch on oxygen, straightened him out carefully, got him on a stretcher, and took off with lights flashing.

"You go home and take care of the kids," said Bill. "I'll go and check on Bullfinch and make sure they take good care of him. And oh—I guess I should get some bandages."

"Yes," she said. "And ask for a priest."

"I'm not going to die."

"Get them to wash those cuts out with holy water."

Bill stared at her, but did not—in the end—object.

Just then, Maddy's phone rang. It was Hildy.

"What the hell was that all about?" she said. "Screaming at me and hanging up... where are you?"

"Are you home?" Maddy asked, ignoring her friend's question. "The kids...?"

"Are right here with me, and yes, at home," Hildy said. "We dropped in on Adam Even, watched a couple of old movies, played with a sword… typical night. It got a little weird at the end, so I cut the visit short. Why?"

"I don't know," Maddy said. "I'll let you know when I get home."

Now, just as she had in her vision, Maddy stood outside Adam Even's door. She'd talked with Hildy for about fifteen minutes and gotten a complete rundown on their visit. Now she was going to do some investigating.

From all reports, most of the evening had gone fine. There had only been that one thing—the cats upstairs at the end. It had felt like it might get weird about then, but it was then that Maddy had called, and after that Adam had cheerfully bid them good-bye. Now they were all home, no problem.

Still, there were those noises. And there was the Noose, and the club. Maddy had a few more questions to ask Adam, and she didn't want the others distracting her—or him.

She'd called his number and gotten no answer. She'd left a message for him to return the call, but she'd heard nothing. She fingered the silver cross necklace she wore now around her neck, sighed, and turned away. She still had her questions, and she thought there might not be much time left. There were other Noose Club members, and one of them was going to talk.

21

She swam before him out of focus.

He felt confused and adrift, as though he'd been underwater for a very long time. It was as if he was wrapped in heavy, wet seaweed and it weighed him down. He struggled toward the surface, toward the light he could just make out.

He started.

Something surrounded him. It was something electric and startling.

The image before him swam into focus.

It was a woman.

"Isabella?" he said in a weak voice.

"Do not exert yourself, Geoffrey. You took quite a fall. Or did you suddenly get the notion that you could fly?"

Bullfinch tingled. Somewhere in his body there was pain, but it felt distant, as if it was on the other side of some fence. All he knew now was that he was lying perpendicular with a handsome woman standing before him.

"I'll get the nurse," Isabella said.

And she was gone, hurrying out of the room. "He is awake; my friend is awake!" she announced excitedly in a mildly accented voice.

For Bullfinch's part, he was at a loss. Where was he? And why was he here? And what was Isabella Ferrara doing here? Last he'd heard, she was off to the Vatican and about to head to the Himalayas in search of some rampaging yeti.

He looked around. It did not take long for him to realize he was in a hospital. To his right was a bank of machines. There were tubes in his arms, and he felt the all-too-familiar touch of a cold catheter. But there was also an unfamiliar touch.

His legs were raised and covered in casts. One of his arms was also encased in plaster. Wires descended from a framework above the bed, dangling his limbs gently, as though he were some sort of oversized puppet.

Good lord! He was in traction!

He held up his free hand. His fingers were wrapped in bandages. He closed his eyes, and flickering visions brought a sudden wash of memory.

Hanging—suspended in space. Nothing but hard cement below. Then…free fall…and a rope around his neck.

The hissing horror…

It still didn't quite connect into a coherent whole, and he had no time to consider it more carefully before a nurse marched in, looking concerned but not displeased. "Well, well, Mr. Bullfinch. Awake?"

"So it would seem," he said.

"Good. We were starting to worry about you. I've called for the doctor. He'll be here presently. Let me take look at your vitals." She was a big woman with a cheerful, smiling face. She started jotting things down on a clip board.

"One-twenty over seventy-nine blood pressure. Pulse… seventy-nine. Excellent, excellent, Mr. Bullfinch. Just stay still and let me finish here."

Bullfinch ignored her and turned to his visitor, raising an eyebrow.

"Hello, Isabella. It's so kind of you to visit," he said. "Unexpected, I'll admit, but kind…"

"Well, she's brought you some kind of luck," the nurse said. "I was figuring on at least another day of unconsciousness for you. It's a pleasure to meet you both. I'm Emily. You want me, you just ring that button there. Oh, and how's your pain? We can give you something if you like."

"I'm not quite sure. Give me a minute."

"Certainly. Well, the doctor will be pleased. I told him not to hurry. You seem to be stable, but don't overtax yourself. We don't want you relapsing, do we? I'll be right outside, like I say."

"Thank you, Emily."

"Water?"

"Well, yes. Come to think of it, I'll have some of that."

Emily returned in a few moments with a glass of chipped ice and held it to Bullfinch's lips. He took a small mouthful and smiled as the ice melted and the liquid trickled down his throat.

"Have to take it slow," Emily said. "Don't want to upset your system." She gave him a second mouthful, then stepped back.

"Do you mind if I spend a little time with my friend now?" Isabella asked. "I can help him with the ice…"

"If he's up to it."

Emily handed the cup to Isabella.

"Well, that's not only restoring, it's cleared my throat." Bullfinch said. "I can speak a bit better. And I heard that. Yes…yes… please… could you give us a few moments, Emily?"

"Very well, then. I shall leave the two of you. The doctor should be here soon."

When she was gone, Bullfinch took a deep breath. "My new friends. Madrigal. The lieutenant captain. Are they—?"

"They're fine, Geoffrey. Mack had all the information on them, and when he heard what happened—you know how quickly he picks up on such things—he contacted me and asked if I could drop in. These friends of yours, it seems, regardless of your current state, that they saved your life."

"No. No, you saved my life! It was you who gave me that huge supply of holy water. Glad I brought some."

"There's a Catholic church here, yes? Holy water is not so hard to find."

"But water blessed by the Holy Father Himself?"

She chuckled. "The pope's underwear goes on one leg at a time. Holy water is holy water. Let's talk business. You fell off a building. A tall one. I'm guessing you didn't jump, so what? You were pushed? Chased? Mack was not so clear on what we're facing here."

"I'm not a hundred percent certain myself," he said. "I wasn't exactly pushed. It got that noose around me—ungodly quick—and sort of forced me over the edge. I think…" he thought for a moment, realizing that as he spoke about it the moment was coming back to him. "I held on there for what seemed a very long time."

"They told me," Isabella said. "They cut the rope on the noose just before…"

Bullfinch closed his eyes again. "Yes. It was close. I would say, all things considered, that falling from that roof as I did was a blessing. Still, the police—Madrigal Harper—they are all in well over their heads, so it's a good thing you were close."

"Close enough. I flew back into New York, but had some time coming and was headed to Los Angeles when Mack called me. You are cutting into my recreation."

Bullfinch laughed.

"I know you better than that… this *is* your recreation… I wish you'd been here with me earlier. I had thought I was facing more of an insubstantial spirit. I'm afraid it caught me absolutely unprepared."

"Perhaps the thing would have scampered away and I would not have been able to enjoy a cup of tea with it, eh?" she showed very white, even teeth in a smile.

The nurse poked her head in.

"The doctor is on his way."

Isabella stood and squeezed his hand. "I will go and find some food, then I'll be back. Then we will talk more of this creature and what we can do. In the meantime," she reached into her pocket and pulled out a small crucifix on a chain, "you must take this. I know you gave yours to the woman. Maddy? You should not be without it until this is done. You, and this thing, are connected now."

Bullfinch closed his hand over the small cross and nodded. He started to smile, but Isabella had already turned and was on her way out the door.

When Isabella returned, Bullfinch was feeling a bit more himself. She pulled a chair up beside the bed and seated herself, giving him a good once over.

"You saw the doctor?"

"Yes. He was very pleased that I was awake. He tells me I'll be in here for a couple of weeks, after which I'll graduate to a wheelchair and physical therapy. With hard work and a little luck, I'll be up and hobbling in a month or two. Good as new in less than a year. He was polite enough not to mention that falling off a roof is not healthy, or that I'm lucky just to be alive."

"I am guessing he also did not mention that you were up against something supernatural, and that, under the circumstances, falling from that roof was your best option."

"He did not."

"I wish that I had been here sooner, my friend," Isabella said.

"It was supposed to be a ghost," Bullfinch said. "I was pretty sure I could handle a ghost…"

"I've been giving that some thought," Isabella said. "I gave your lieutenant captain a call, and asked some questions of my own. I believe it *was* a ghost… but not *just* a ghost."

"Do you want to give me that in Italian or Latin so I can understand it better?"

"I'm surprised it hasn't come to you," she said, almost smiling, despite his injuries. "You really have no idea what it is you were up against?"

"No. Some sort of creature—ugly as sin! Ghost-dwarf? Gnome?"

"Good guess, but…no." She smiled and her eyes sparkled with anticipation. "I believe what you have here is a goblin."

"Goblin?"

"Yes. A goblin. You know that famous painting, *Incubus Sitting on Sleeping Beauty*?"

"I am familiar with it."

"Goblins. They are creatures of faerie—but sometimes the walls between worlds— are not sound."

"And that's why they are like ghosts?"

"Yes, but still very different. Real ghosts avoid them. Goblins eat ghosts for breakfast. They gain a kind of spiritual energy from the consumption of any sort of spirit. And while spirit is strongest in the living, they cannot merely absorb it like vampires suck blood. They must kill it, or have it killed in a certain way so that they can assimilate it. With ghosts... it is much simpler. I have dealt with a goblin before—once."

"That would explain the ectoplasm," Bullfinch said, brow furrowed, "and the speed. That thing moved like lightning. And there were others present, the spirits of a man—and a woman. Something happened on that roof..."

"Hmm. Speed, you say?"

"Yes. Very fast."

Isabella's gaze grew distant, thoughtful.

"No, no," she said to herself, shaking her head. "That's just a myth. A story. Mythology is your territory. Goblins though, they're real enough."

Bullfinch ignored her unfinished thought.

"But, from what I know of goblins, they are almost exclusively European. What would one be doing here in the Pacific Northwest?"

"They are nomadic. They like to travel, and they don't stay in one place for long. When they *do* stay in one place, though, that is trouble."

"Clearly."

"And you say...this one is dwarfish?"

"And ugly. It's almost difficult to look at it. I wonder if that's why it tried, at first, to wear the spirit of a dead woman."

"Ugly yes. They tend to be green, the goblins, with thatches of dark matted hair and sharp, crooked teeth that stick out of their mouths. I have heard that some can transform, so I'm sure yours—no, ours—was putting on a show. You see, what we face here is a creature of high intellect and deep cunning. A being with an agenda."

"Agenda?"

"Yes. A plan. A plan of great mischief. We are a sort of cattle to them, as are our ghosts. They feed on spirits, but those of the living are more nourishing to them—the shells are just harder to crack."

Bullfinch rubbed his temple and tried to think. "It's coming back. They are called kobolds in Germany, true?"

"Yes. They say that some of them worked with Hitler's Nazis, but I find this doubtful. A lot of magical powers were attributed to that man, but in the end he was sad and evil. In any case, I believe that we have one here, and I mean to fight it. It is an abomination."

Bullfinch chuckled, then cut it off. Isabella had worked for the Vatican, and she had strong beliefs. She was a "kill first and don't worry about the questions" kind of agent, and it was good to avoid her bad side.

"You've encountered them before?"

"A minor one. This seems much stronger, more focused."

She reached out and tucked a folded sheet of paper in his hand.

"We will talk soon. I am going to do some exploring, perhaps ask a few more questions. I have not yet met this Madrigal Harper, or her son, and I would like to talk with one of those who possess the nooses."

Bullfinch frowned at the paper, and when he looked up she was simply gone.

"I hate that," he muttered. Then he unfolded the paper and began to read.

It was a poem by Christina Rossetti.

THE GOBLIN MARKET

Morning and evening
Maids heard the goblins cry:
"Come buy our orchard fruits,
Come buy, come buy:
Apples and quinces,
Lemons and oranges,
Plump unpeck'd cherries,
Melons and raspberries,
Bloom-down-cheek'd peaches,
Swart-headed mulberries,
Wild free-born cranberries,
Crab-apples, dewberries,
Pine-apples, blackberries,
Apricots, strawberries;—
All ripe together
In summer weather,—
Morns that pass by,
Fair eves that fly;
Come buy, come buy:
Our grapes fresh from the vine,
Pomegranates full and fine,
Dates and sharp bullaces,
Rare pears and greengages,
Damsons and bilberries,
Taste them and try:
Currants and gooseberries,
Bright-fire-like barberries,
Figs to fill your mouth,
Citrons from the South,
Sweet to tongue and sound to eye;
Come buy, come buy."

22

The goblin known as Robin Redcap was reading aloud from an ancient book. In fact, he was just finishing up "The Goblin Market" for Adam Even. The Goblin read in a thick, Scottish brogue...

Golden head by golden head,
Laugh'd every goblin
When they spied her peeping:
Came towards her hobbling,
Flying, running, leaping,
Puffing and blowing,
Chuckling, clapping, crowing,
Clucking and gobbling,
Mopping and mowing,
Full of airs and graces,
Pulling wry faces,
Demure grimaces,
Cat-like and rat-like,
Ratel- and wombat-like,
Snail-paced in a hurry,
Parrot-voiced and whistler,
Helter skelter, hurry skurry,

Redcap stopped, cackled, and leaned in closer. "Pay attention. This is where I got that inspiration for The Beatles and that most delightful of humans, my dear, dear pal, Charlie Manson!"

He continued while Adam Even listened, head in hands.

Lashing their tails
They trod and hustled her,
Elbow'd and jostled her,
Claw'd with their nails,
Barking, mewing, hissing, mocking,
Tore her gown and soil'd her stocking,
Twitch'd her hair out by the roots,
Stamp'd upon her tender feet,
Held her hands and squeez'd their fruits
Against her mouth to make her eat.
White and golden Lizzie stood,
Like a lily in a flood,—
Like a rock of blue-vein'd stone

"Ooh. Good stuff. I did a bloody good job with these nine-teen-century poets and writers, didn't I?"

"And tell them of her early prime,
Those pleasant days long gone
Of not-returning time:
Would talk about the haunted glen,
The wicked, quaint fruit-merchant men,
Their fruits like honey to the throat
But poison in the blood;
(Men sell not such in any town):
Would tell them how her sister stood
In deadly peril to do her good,
And win the fiery antidote:
Then joining hands to little hands
Would bid them cling together,
"For there is no friend like a sister
In calm or stormy weather;
To cheer one on the tedious way,
To fetch one if one goes astray,
To lift one if one totters down,
To strengthen whilst one stands."

The goblin closed the book and grinned. "Aye! Nice, then, eh?"

"Very," said Adam.

"You cannae tell me women cannae scribble a bit from time to time. And aye—a splendid first edition as well." The goblin got up from his chair at the table and hobbled over to a shelf where he reinserted the book carefully. He scratched his behind with his long, ragged fingernails as he examined more of the books. "And these be the books for the bairns, then? But "The Goblin Market" was never a poem for children. Now, "The Princess and the Goblin" by George MacDonald. That was for children, aye. Though I daresay no children read it these days —" His wild green eyes lit up beneath his thatch of coarse black hair. "And bloody well good, I say!"

23

Bullfinch glanced up as the door to his room opened, and smiled. The man standing there was tall, athletic, with quick eyes that darted everywhere at once, while still managing to maintain contact—taking in everything. He carried a bag over one shoulder and when he saw Geoffrey, his grin widened.

"Mack!" Bullfinch said. "What on earth are *you* doing here? I was surprised to see Isabella, but how in the world did you convince R.C. to cut you loose?"

"He's in Greece," Mack said. "Rebecca is keeping an eye on things. I have to get out of there now and then or go crazy. Besides, I had to see for myself if it was true that you'd taken to inner-city cliff-diving. Looks like I'm lucky to find you alive."

"I've been better," Bullfinch said. "And worse. I'm afraid I'm not going to be much good for field work for a while, though…"

"Have feet, will travel," Mack said. "Give me a minute here, have to check in. Leaving HQ is one thing, going off the grid is another."

"Of course," Bullfinch said. "I'm sure the hospital has a Wi-Fi connection…"

Mack raised an eyebrow and shook his head.

"Not for me, they don't," he said. They are only running one hundred and twenty-eight-bit encryption, and the password for their network is the name of the street out front and their phone number. I'll trust my own connection, thanks."

He flipped open a laptop and plugged a small box into it. There were a number of colored lights on the side of the box, and they began blinking rapidly as Mack powered up the machine. A moment later, his eyes were glued to the screen, and his fingers flying over the keys.

Finally satisfied with whatever he'd been checking, he glanced up. Bullfinch noted that the young man's fingers continued to tap the keys, even as he spoke. Every moment or two, he glanced down, though he did not seem distracted.

"Magic," Bullfinch muttered.

"Hardly," Mack said. "Is Isabella here? I didn't see her on the way in…"

"She's got her own methods," Bullfinch said. "She wanted to do some investigation of her own…"

"Fine. I'll call her in a minute. I want to compare some notes here."

He glanced down at the screen again.

"I've been in touch with Madrigal Harper. Fine investigator. Facts. Data. She can dig them out. Ah, here we go." He turned the screen around. "It seems that, after some careful digging, we've discovered a connection that was missed before. Had to go back pretty far, and Maddy has been busy, calling around and interviewing homeowners and realtors… All of the stories have one thing in common, and we've even lucked into a single photo to back it up."

Bullfinch stared down at the screen. What he saw appeared to be a woman, a very old, sort of piggy-looking woman with a snout of a nose and a toss of ratty scraggly hair that looked more stitched on than growing from her scalp. She was stout, broad in the shoulders, and about as attractive as a junkyard dog. For all of that, she was dressed in very nice clothing—no makeup, but well-dressed. Expensively dressed.

She had on an expansive New York style hat and was wearing a gorgeous French raincoat, the kind that older women like Meryl Streep looked so good in.

She was smiling too. And one of her teeth was gold.

Her eyes gleamed.

"Who is she?" Bullfinch asked.

"Unless I miss my guess," Mack said, "she's the one making the rounds and dropping off those nooses causing all the trouble. She's been a figure in local real estate, behind the scenes, for decades. No one seems to know her name, but they can describe her. They know they've seen her. They verify she's been connected with the homes that, eventually, produced the nooses."

"Something about that picture," Bullfinch said. He frowned. "There's something that bothers me, but I can't quite put my finger on it—something I should remember."

"I expected that it might," Mack said. "You know me—I didn't stop with this image. Once I had it, I ran it through several facial recognition algorithms. First I went back a decade, then two, and then I pulled out the stops. I got exactly one hit. Here."

He tapped on his keyboard and showed Bullfinch the results.

Bullfinch stared, and the hairs on his arms slowly stood, a sensation like hundreds of tiny ants crossing his skin sent an uncontrollable shiver through him, shaking his leg in its traction.

It was an old picture, a painting actually, and the colors had faded.

"Oh, good heavens."

"You recognize her."

"Good Lord," Bullfinch gasped. "It's Alison Gross. The ugliest witch in the North Country!"

"Who?" Mack seemed taken aback.

"It's a very old legend. Most would say she's only a myth."

Before Bullfinch had fully processed what he'd seen, Mack was back at the keyboard. "There's a folk song about her," he said. "The most recent version is by a group called Steeleye Span. I'm familiar with them—very old music with an electric feel to it."

He tapped the keys, turned up his volume, and a haunting melody poured out of the tiny speakers. The two listened in silence for a moment, then Mack broke that silence.

"This song is about a witch," he said. "I thought we'd already determined that the creature you tangled with was some form of goblin?"

"There is no clear information on who, or what Gross might have been," Bullfinch said thoughtfully. "In those days, before the Internet and data grids, information was dependent on memory and understanding, and tainted by the beliefs and facts available to historians or folklorists. There is no telling whether she might be that creature, or whether the two might be working together, or one for the other. There is no denying one thing—the stakes have been raised."

Mack continued to tap on his keyboard as he listened, frowning. He shook his head. "Sorry, Bullfinch. I do better with UFOs."

"In this case, I don't believe we're going to have to search your precious databases for a connection," Bullfinch said. "You might say, the two of them go way back."

"Huh?"

"The stories about both connect," Bullfinch said. "Their paths have crossed, so to speak, and I see no reason to believe that it might not be happening again... though—as I said—it might *not* be."

"I see. Well. Hmm. Well...have you seen this...this witch goblin?"

"No. And that bothers me."

"Why? Maybe she doesn't even exist?"

"We have proof that you just showed me that a woman who looks very much like her painting was seen in the vicinity of the haunted nooses. And now it would seem that the goblin is reaping the harvest. When I confronted that creature, and it forced me off the roof, it pretended to be a spirit haunting that building. It drew me into the role of another such spirit, and it spoke to me. Once we fought back, and that hold began to fade, it said something... something about needing me... needing to absorb me."

Mack frowned. He did another quick search.

"It's commonly believed that such creatures feed off of human souls," Mack said. "At least among those who believe such things exist. But why, if it's so powerful, go to all the trouble to feed only through the nooses? And what is the connection with Gross?"

"Very good questions," Bullfinch replied. "And questions we'll need to get answered quickly. I don't believe that our presence is going to do anything to prevent further killings—we're going to have to take the battle to it—or them—and do it soon."

Mack powered down the laptop and stowed it quickly.

"I'm going out to see if I can track down Isabella. You get some rest—I'm afraid that nurse outside will skin me alive if I keep you up any longer. I'll let you know what we find, and we'll come up with a plan of action. I know that will make Isabella happy."

"If we don't, she'll act anyway," Bullfinch chuckled. "She's not much for the subtle approach."

Mack took Bullfinch's good hand and shook it, then turned, and was gone as quickly as he'd appeared.

Bullfinch stared at the door a moment longer, brow furrowed. Then he closed his eyes and tried his best not to conjure the image of that squat, ugly woman, or the thing he'd faced on the hotel roof.

24

Vincent "Vinnie" Malone travelled a hell of a lot. Far too much for his taste. He would, in fact, be far happier back in his hometown of Teaneck, New Jersey, doing fuck all. Things had changed. You couldn't roll into a town and roll up to a joint where the guys were connected. Everyone was so far underground it was hard to tell from day to day who worked for whom.

That's why he'd gotten into this home improvement gig. It wasn't hard work, really. And Vinnie, he had the gift of gab. He worked for a nice cutlery and cookery outfit, and what Vinnie did was put on cooking demonstrations.

Vinnie was good at that, and he knew it.

"You oughta have your own fuckin' show, Vincenco!" the boss would say, after seeing one of his demos down in a show in Newark. "To hell with all these other mooks. I'm watching and laughin' and then I'm eatin' and I'm grinnin'."

"That's awful nice of you to say, sir," Vinnie had said. "Only thing is, I gotta travel with this shit. And be away from, you know, wife and bambinos."

Wife and bambinos, yeah. And a hot lovin' babe down in Hackensack. Maria, Little Vincent, and Lucretia he could do without for long stretches.

But Teaneck! Teaneck and Hilda! Teaneck and Bischoff's Ice Cream, and Rollins Newsstand and even the bagel shop for Christ's sake.

This place here, though—Eugene, Oregon. Wasn't so bad!

If fact, it kinda reminded him of Teaneck, what with the old houses and the old "ain't gonna change, buster" feel. Not a town that had been planned to be "urban," and with lots and lots of trees.

Vinnie, he liked trees. He enjoyed the trees as he walked up from his motel room on 7th to the Lane County Fairgrounds where the Lane County Home Improvement Show was happening. All scrubbed up and ready to go. Hadn't a drop last night, no sir. Today was the big day. Friday was always the most important, to get the lay of the land, the cut of the community jib. After that, in the evening, he could go to a bar, drink, pick up some broad and be good for the rest of the weekend.

Trees! Yes, and a nice fall day. Supposed to be rainy as hell here, but what he'd been hearing from the locals as he'd set up the day before was that summer had been dry as a bone, and the fall had been golden—but not enough damned water!

Well screw 'em, thought Vinnie. *They can die of dehydration. I'll be back in Bergen County, baby, where we got enough water we don't have to buy it at freakin' stores!*

Friday went very well. Suckers! These hicks were the biggest suckers in the world!

Hell, Vinnie thought, *maybe the West Coast wasn't so bad. Note to self, Pacific Northwest. Regular visits.*

On his way back to the motel, though, he decided to be a tourist. He hung a right on 13th, scooted on down to Olive, and swung past a nice big Catholic church. He hung a right on 10th and checked out the library. It was a nice, clean building. Not like some of the neighborhood libraries back east. Across the street was the local Community College.

There was a cop station there, but he ignored it. Nothing to worry about on this trip, he was clean. Too clean in his opinion. Man, he'd done some serious shit in his day, and if the law had caught him, his ass would still be in jail.

Down to the right of Broadway, past lots of bums with dogs looking like ol' pothead Bill Sykes' Dickens characters was a bar called the Stardust, advertising "Happy Hour Martinis."

He went in. Almost empty. He waved to the bartender. "Gin, please!"

"Dirty?"

"Oh, yeah!"

Vinnie liked his martinis dirty, which meant with some olive jar juice added.

The guy poured from a bottle that's label proclaimed it to be "Crater Lake" gin, some sort of local spirit.

And who'd have guessed? It was fantastic.

Stirred like he asked for. Four huge olives. A fancy glass.

And only three bucks.

Three freakin' bucks!

Back in Jersey, these bushwhackers would have set him back six bucks. In Manhattan, eight.

He knocked one back and smiled. "That's good, fella." He put a buck on the bar, and then pulled out his wallet.

"Another please."

The next one he took his time with, dragging it over to the light and grabbing the local free paper, the *Eugene Weekly*.

There was plenty going on. Vinnie noticed a club called The Jazz Station, and smiled. It was just around the corner. Maybe if he didn't get too smashed on the cheap gin, he'd go and check that place out.

The evening had taken on a different hue as Vinnie felt good when he left the bar. Everything had darkened and deepened. The sky was bluer than any he could ever remember seeing, and the clouds seemed so close he might reach out and touch them. He wondered if maybe the local hippies put something extra in that gin. He was crossing the next street, 8th Ave, when he saw it.

It was over on the other side of Olive St. along with a couple of other food carts. One seemed to be for Southern style cooking, while the other sold vegetarian food.

It was the sign that caught Vinnie's eye:

NEW JERSEY PIZZA—the Real Stuff.

When Vinnie saw that, he stopped in the middle of the street.

It took a honk of a horn to get his ass moving again.

Are you kidding me? he thought.

Safe across the street, he squinted at the cart.

Yep. That's what it said, all right. New Jersey pizza.

Yeah. He thought. *Right.*

Pizza slices, plain, just cheese, were only $2.50.

Vinnie thought, *Shit, I can spare that and then spit the rest out when I don't like it.*

There was a young boy who looked like a college student at the cart's window. Vinnie ordered a slice.

Paid.

It was served on a cheap, white paper plate. Just like back home.

He sniffed at it suspiciously. Hmm. Looked like it had enough oregano. He went over and sat down at a communal picnic table.

Here's how you eat a slice, you rubes, he thought as he watched a guy eating two pepperoni numbers with a knife and fork. *You take it like so, fold it like so, and eat it from the skinny part up.*

He took the folded slice and stuck a few inches in his mouth. Bit it off. Chewed.

"Oh, Jesus," said Vinnie, reverently.

Magic!

There it was. Good pizza wasn't just flour and cheese and tomatoes. It was good, quality ingredients in the right proportions, with the perfect spices, and baked in the right way.

It all came together in his mouth, exploding in an oregano opera. Just hot enough too. It was like something he'd get down on Cedar Lane on a good day, when Tony was cooking.

He scarfed the rest down and got another piece. Sausage. It was perfect, and homemade, not those rat pellet turds they served on chain pizzas.

He was just finishing the second slice when he heard a woman's voice.

"We doin' okay on the parmesan?"

"Yeah, I think so."

"What, you don't know? Let me have a look. Jesus, kid, there's practically none left." The boy put it in a little oven, heated it up. "And whassa matter with you?" said the woman. "You're almost outta napkins."

"Oh, yeah!"

"What, people gonna eat my pizza without napkins? I don't think so. Now I gotta go back to the restaurant."

"Sorry."

"Sheesh. I gotta watch you like a hawk. Like a hawk! From now on, you check inventory and tell me before I come out here with the pies. That way, no extra trip."

"Yes, ma'am."

Vinnie recognized the voice. He couldn't believe it. Her? Out here. What the hell?

Carefully, keeping his coat collar up, Vinnie peered around.

Sure enough, it was her. Lynn Mancuso. And damn, if she still wasn't smokin' hot. Better than when he'd dated her, back in the '90s.

Vinnie quickly returned his attention to his slice, or rather what was left of it.

He nibbled at the cooling crust, thinking.

Lynn, she'd married Ralphie, that clown. Yeah, there were lots of guys between him and Ralphie, but still he felt jealous. He always got that twinge of a broken heart when he looked at her or thought about her. She had that dark, searing hot Neopolitan look to her that said, *Paisano. You like?*

So Ralphie was out here with her, then, and they had a restaurant. They'd brought decent pizza to this podunk town. But what the hell was Ralphie...

And then he remembered.

Holy Mary Mother of God! Ralphie had gotten himself in way deep on loans. And no, we weren't talking about Cousin Nunzio or Nephew Thomaso putting up a few g's with a nice round vigorish.

He waited. He bided his time. He nibbled on his crust.

Lynn, she didn't know he was alive. She sure didn't notice him here now.

She did her stuff, harangued the help a bit more, and then carried some boxes of stuff out to a Volvo station wagon parked not far away.

Vinnie watched all this, as best he could. He didn't figure she'd recognized him, after all these years. But you couldn't be too careful.

After the Volvo putted off in a spume of polite pollution, Vinnie dumped his paper plate and some damned cold crust and he jockeyed over to the hired help.

Christ. He's stumbled onto someone on the run from the freaking mob… He had to think about this for a minute.

"Man, that was good pizza!" he said, dabbing at his lips with a napkin.

"Glad you liked it." Kid looked preoccupied. And no wonder.

"I did. And you know what? I couldn't help but overhear your conversation a few minutes ago. So that's your boss, huh?"

"Yes."

"That bitch sounds like she's from the East Coast!"

He brightened a bit. "I guess so. People around here are sure easier to work with. I'm lookin' for a new gig myself. Man. And her husband…"

"Those East Coast bastards are really hard to take, huh?"

That caught the guy up short. "Well, I don't know. They're just on a different wavelength or something. I mean, we're all human beings, right?"

Vinnie laughed. "Yeah. You're a good kid. What, you go to the U. of O. here?"

"Yes. I'm majoring in Architecture."

"Excellent. Excellent! You know what, my friend?"

"No. What?"

"You got a whole world ahead of you. And you'll always remember—in college, you had better pizza than folks at Stanford, UCA, UCLA, and… what's that other college you Ducks hate?"

The kid smiled. "Oh, we don't hate any of them. We just want to beat the shit out of them!"

Vinnie almost choked, he started laughing so hard.

"Yeah. I like the Ducks, too! But I like pizza and this is good pizza and from what I hear, that babe that was bustin' your balls, she has a restaurant where she cooks this good pizza. Now where would that be, pray tell?"

The kid brightened. "Yeah… they have all kinds of food there, not just the pizza. My favorite is the baked ziti."

"Great… can you point me in the right direction?"

"Oh. Right. It's over on West Eighteenth. In the shopping strip right across from Churchill High School."

"Okay. So… if you were going to explain that to someone obviously *not* from here…"

The kid gave him directions and a business card.

"It's called 'Mama's Best Italian'. Can't miss it."

"Thanks." He gave the kid five bucks.

"Wow. Thank *you*. Tell 'em I sent you."

He gave the kid another five bucks.

"Don't mention we talked, okay?"

The kid looked puzzled as hell. But he took the money.

Another thing about Eugene. Vinnie found a payphone. Try and find one of *those* still working back east. He dropped his change, waited.

"What," a voice answered, sounding bored, or tired.

"Marty, it's Vinnie. Listen, you're gonna want to hear this. Okay. So I'm in this town called Eugene."

"Eugene? Sounds gay."

"It's pretty happy, yeah. But listen. This is why I'm callin', Marty. Remember Ralphie? The guy on the lam from the big guys?"

"I remember. He owed 'em a hundred grand easy, and that was years ago. With interest…he must owe 'em a million by now."

"There a hit out for him?"

"Naw. What the fuck! This ain't Godfatherville no more. Bosses sure would like to see some of that money, though."

"So I found him."

"Found who?"

"Well, I think I found him. Ralphie."

"No shit. So what?"

"He's got an operation here."

"Where's 'here'?"

"Eugene! I told you."

"Oh, yeah. The gay place. What kind of operation?"

"Restaurants."

"You seen the place?"

"I seen the food cart that goes with it. Ate there. Good pizza."

"Hmm. Yeah. I see where you're going with this. Someone we know may …ah…want a taste of that pizza."

"And he'd appreciate me a bit more then too, huh?"

"Whuh? Oh shit. He's always liked you. But things aren't exactly shakin' lately. Know what I mean?"

"I'm out here in the heartland hawkin' cookware! I know what you mean!"

They both got a laugh out of that.

"Okay. Yeah, I'd say he'd be interested. Why don't you go check it out?"

"I'm on it. And thanks!"

He hung up, and grinned.

Vinnie found the restaurant right where the kid had said he would. It was tucked between an All-Nite Donuts and a Mexican joint. Mama's. Mama's Best Italian kitchen.

He calmed down.

He went back to his Spark. He sat behind the wheel and turned on the radio. KRVM was playing the blues. Sounded good. Vinnie rolled down the window and stuck his head out.

He took in a deep breath of the clean air, tried to center his thoughts, and then reached beneath his seat and took his gun out. It was a cheap, snub-nose thingie. He wasn't clear on the caliber, but he knew that it could put a hole in a guy, and that was all that really mattered. It was loaded and he thumbed the safety off.

He got out and walked past the restaurant.

Yep. There she was. Lynn.

There was an older couple in the restaurant. She had her ticket book and was busy filling it out. She was smiling. Yeah, she looked so much better when she was smiling, no question about that.

There wasn't anyone at the front, where there was a big display of menu items. He walked on down to the little gym. He wasted time looking at a couple of ads in windows for upcoming shows at local music venues. When he was certain no one had seen him, he turned and walked back.

Bingo. When he passed the restaurant again, he saw him. Unmistakable. He'd shaved off his mustache and had cut his greasy black hair short, but there was no question about it. It was Ralphie.

Vinnie reached into his pocket and felt for his gun.

It was hard and cold in his hand.

He smiled to himself, and released the grip. He was glad it wasn't just on him. There were other ways to do this.

"Yeah," Vinnie said. "There's no question. It's him."

"It's Ralphie."

"And he's got two restaurants?"

"Pretty much."

"Hmmm. You see, the boss is pissed. But he'd rather get some money than kill the guy, know what I mean? But Ralphie, he don't know that. That's why he's on the lam. Too bad."

"I don't know. I guess I could lean on him."

There was a bark of laughter. "You? Hah! You couldn't lean on a leg of lamb. No, I remembered we got a guy out in Seattle. You know Chomp, don't you?"

"The big guy with the scar?"

"Yep. He keeps fit and he works sometimes at the club. Bouncer, you know."

"I remember him. Jeez, that guy has shoulders than can hold up the Tappan Zee Bridge."

"Yeah, and he can do all kinds of jobs, if you get my drift."

"Well, listen. Sometimes, Chomp doesn't hurt anyone. He just shows up, he frowns and growls a bit and scratches his balls, if you know what I mean, and people pay up!"

"And this guy's in Seattle?"

"He's finished and visiting a relative. He can be on the plane day after tomorrow."

Vinnie smiled. "That works! I'll be finished up here with my gig. But look…I'm still gonna get a finder's fee?"

"Oh, yeah. And I bet the boss will want you to have dinner with him. Talk about things, huh?"

Vinnie grinned. Oh, yeah. That was what he wanted to hear. Better than money. Getting back in the trenches with his buddy soldiers. That was a lot more fun that hawkin' cookware, any day of the week!

"You got my number!"

"Right. We'll call you tomorrow and give you the details."

"Great."

"Oh, and Vinnie. Don't show yourself, huh? Don't wanna scare off the marks."

"I gotcha."

When Vinnie got back into his rental car he was still grinning.

25

The old woman went into Starbucks and asked for a Venti tea with English Breakfast Black.

When she received it, she shook her head and clucked her tongue. "My my, this is not boiled water. Boiling water brings out tea's flavor you know?" She had an English accent. Yorkshire, to be specific. "I wonder if you might microwave it for minute. Just till it boils?"

"I'm sorry, ma'am. Can't do that!" said the annoyed barista, wiping his hand on his napkin.

"Oh, dear. I always forget that I live here among the barbarians. No matter. I shall suffer in silence."

Her shoulders slumped and she took her tea over to the prep table. There she poured some full cream milk in, along with four packets of white sugar. Then she found a table well to the back, where the Wi-Fi signal would be stronger.

As she waited for her Mac Air to power up, she held the cup of tea in her hand, grimaced a bit.

And then smiled.

A puff of steam sailed out of the slot in the top.

As she let it steep, she got online and checked her email.

This. That. Another... So many chores! But such fun, such, such fun.

Some people might have called her a crone. She was quite wrinkled, her nose was long and her hair was straggly. She wore no makeup, but she wore good-quality clothes and smelled like English roses in spring. She liked that smell. It reminded her of home and old times.

She checked her usual websites, and then she checked her email.

The one she was interested in most, the reason she was here in Eugene, Oregon, again, was there.

An address.

And:

"Beware!"

Oh, yes, she would beware, she thought, wrapping her scarf around her throat. She looked at the sunset. It was bleeding out over the horizon, puce and crimson. Human blood from a pierced artery.

She smiled to herself.

She had always liked the sunsets in Oregon.

26

Vinnie picked Chomp up at the Eugene Airport.

Best damned airport Vinnie had ever seen. Mahlon Sweet, the place was called, and boy, it was just that. Sweet. Easy to get into. Easy to get out of. Cheap parking. Pleasant facilities.

So pleasant, in fact, that on the late morning of Chomp's arrival, Vinnie enjoyed himself sitting at the beer bar of the restaurant, drinking one of the excellent local microbrews, which was cheap as hell compared to what they charged back in New Jersey and New York. He was on his second when Chomp finally came down the escalator.

Vinnie met him at the gate.

"Chomp! Welcome to Eugene, Oregon! You got bags?"

Chomp wasn't the quickest of guys, but he was careful. He looked at Vinnie for a minute. *So long,* Vinnie thought he heard gears grinding. Then Chomp smiled in recognition. "Oh, yeah! I know you."

"Sure you do."

"What the hell are you doing out here?"

"Same as you. Workin', Chomp."

"Oh, yeah. Workin'. Listen, my name his Herman, Herman Chompksi. Mr. Chompski to you, for now. You got that?"

He pounded Vinnie on a shoulder and Vinnie almost fell over. He managed to keep his feet, and nodded.

"You got a car?"

"Mr. Chompski, with you I got an expense account."

Chomp looked at him, really looked at him, for the first time. A big smile broke out on that big face.

Twenty minutes later, they were sitting in a booth with two more of the local beers. Chomp was halfway through his when he said, "That was just a swallow. I'm having another. What is this stuff?"

"Ninkasi."

"Some Russian brew?"

"No, it's local. They brew a lot of beer here in Eugene."

"What the hell," Chomp said, gulping what remained in his bottle. "Give me another."

Vinnie grinned. He waved the waitress over and placed the order. He only ordered one.

"I got to drive," he said. "I'll get another one later on."

Chompski smiled. "Whatever. So, Ralphie, huh?"

"You remember Ralphie?"

"Not so much. I remember his broad though."

"Yeah, me, too. In any case, it's Ralphie that owes."

Chompski smiled. "Maybe the broad owes, too."

Vinnie thought about that. He didn't know how to take it.

Then he said, "So, you got a feelin' for that broad? You date her or somethin'?"

Chompski took a big long sigh. For a heartbeat he actually looked human. "No. I'm kinda shy."

"Oh."

"That was a seriously good brewski," Chomp said, finishing his second. "Gimme another."

"Well... Are you sure?"

"Look. I had a hard time with my uncle. Capiche? I'm gettin' happy now. Okay? You okay with that, Vinnie?"

"Well, yeah, sure, of course."

"What? We gotta put the move on this guy tonight?"

"No. I was thinking tomorrow."

"Yep. You think right." He snapped his fingers. "Another of these. He's paying, sister. And he's driving."

The waitress looked Chomp up and down and laughed. "I don't know. Eugene police may not want to deal with you."

That brought a big smile to Chomp's face. "Thanks. That's

funny. Ain't that funny, Vinnie?"

"That's funny. I'm fine though."

Chomp sat and sipped his beer. Vinnie watched and grinned. He didn't know the guy, and he didn't trust him not to go south and pound him, but still... it was good to talk to someone from back home.

Vinnie barely slept that night. He was through with his cookery gig. All packed up and ready to roll out, but he was still wired over the whole Ralphie thing.

Chomp was a professional. He radiated mastery.

You want someone dead?

Get Chomp.

You want someone intimidated?

Definitely get Chomp.

So, all Vinnie had to do then was to stand back, tip his hat to all concerned, smile and take his credit.

Right.

Yeah, right. Sure.

Still, something bothered him. And he wasn't quite sure what.

Maybe it had something to do with the nightmares he'd been having.

He watched some TV, then watched the door, wishing the day would start, or end, or that he'd never called back east, or that he had some damn pizza.

At three-thirty PM, there was a knock on his door.

He opened it. Outside was Chomp, looking bright, healthy and freakin' BIG.

He looked today like Triple H from WWE Wrestling, his long hair tucked back behind his head, his chest big, his shoulders wide. He was wearing a respectable suit, but was clearly no one to mess with.

"I'm ready," said Vinnie. He'd tucked his gun into a holster under a jacket.

"This will be easy," said Chomp.

"I hope," said Vinnie.

Quietly they walked down to the car and got in.

Vinnie headed toward the restaurant. It was about a twelve-minute ride, and while Vinnie drove, Chomp started talking.

"Okay, listen up. I'm in charge here. I'm your boss."

"Sure."

"We just want Ralphie. Let's not fuck with the wife."

"Sure."

"We got to get him away from his place. You keep your mouth shut. I'll do the talkin'. He knows you, right?"

"Yeah."

"What I need from you is some fire in your eyes. Think you can do that? What I want is for you to think about Ralphie. How many times he fucked your old girlfriend."

"Hell. You know about that?"

"I made a few calls. I know stuff now. It's all good."

"Okay."

"Fire in your eyes. I want you to look at him and I want you to see him hangin' by his balls over a slow-cookin' fire. Got it?"

Vinnie said, "Yeah. Got it. I think I can do that."

"Good."

"We take Ralphie out to the park next door. We put him down on a bench. We talk to him. I don't think there will be a problem after that."

"Sounds simple."

"Simple is best. But I ain't simple. I may look fuckin' stupid. I'm not."

They drove for a while in silence.

"Thanks for comin' down, Chomp. I couldn't have done this myself."

"I know."

27

Ralphie didn't see the car with his old pals from Jersey pull into the parking lot and slot itself between a couple of SUVs.

He had other things on his mind.

First, he had to cook some stuff. Not bad. All he had to do was to stick the pans in the oven. Lynn had fixed them earlier. Stuff flew out the door in the evening and you had to get it ready now. He'd told April to not come in until five today. She was the waitress and kitchen help, a cute college kid. Good worker too, and pulled in some nice tips, good for her and all that.

Also, today he had to go over to see Phil at his house. Phil had some money for him. Next week was the trip to Vegas and boy, that was gonna be great. Ralphie knew that when Phil was in the mood to give him some money, he had to pick it up before the guy changed his mind. One of the things he was putting in the oven, in fact, was a special Phil's Chicago Pie he was gonna bring over, hot as sin, juicy and dripping.

Vegas! Geez! He could feel the dice in his hands. He could hear them clicking as he rattled them in an open palm, threw… and there! Look! Fuck! Eight? And there came his money! Pouring in, those chips just pouring in.

And there was Lynn beside him, eyes bright and hazed with alcohol and a snort of coke, clapping and screeching.

Gonna be a hot night TOO-NIGHT!

The smells of fresh oregano, good dough, and a garlic hung in the restaurant like aromatic promises. Ralphie was singing.

"Don't stop believin'!" He was off key, of course, but to himself he sounded like Steve Perry in Journey.

That was when the bells jingled.

He was bent over an oven and he stood up, smiling. A customer! Pennies from heaven.

Two men walked in. They did not look like they'd walked in from Eugene, Oregon. No, these two men looked as though they'd taken a door from an alternate universe that was all northern New Jersey and stepped through into this one.

"Yo!"

Ralphie said nothing. He just looked.

At first he didn't recognize either of these guys.

But he didn't have to recognize them, not really. They smelled and looked like stuff right out of his worst nightmares.

What he'd been dreading.

This was what was what in the top of Ralphie's head. His body felt paralyzed. The only thing he could make work, characteristically, was his mouth.

"Yo," he said. "What's up? You guys want some good pizza?"

The monster stepped up to the Formica bar. Without warning, an arm—a long arm—shot out and grabbed Ralphie by the top of his shirt, the exact spot where he couldn't wiggle out from. With huge power, Ralphie found himself being pulled against the counter. In just a second he went from a guy standing in his restaurant to a guy lying on the counter of his restaurant like a flopping fish pulled from a pizza sea.

"Ralphie, you're comin' with us. You say a freakin' word, I'm tearin' off your head and sticking it where there's no sun. Capiche?"

Ralphie looked up and in a terrified but lucid moment. He was looking at the other guy, not as big but just as scary.

"Vinnie," he said.

Vinnie said no more than what his eyes had to say. He reached over and together he and the other guy pulled Ralphie over the counter.

Somewhere along the way Ralphie found a fist in his gut, pounding out air.

"So, Ralphie. Gonna throw up? Do it now."

Ralphie didn't throw up. Ralphie didn't do anything. He just hung like Jesus crucified in the arms of his captors.

"Okay. The park," said the big man.

Ralphie didn't know what was going on. One moment he was dragged over the counter by a big guy, next he was punched, next he was being dragged out onto the sidewalk outside of Mama's Best Italian Kitchen.

The guys who were dragging him didn't say squat, and neither did Ralphie. In fact, he realized that what he was doing wasn't being dragged. He was walking. He managed to lift his head. There was no one else around. The parking lot was empty.

"Hurry up," said the big man.

"Okay, Ralphie, baby. One step two step. Make it easier on yourself."

Oh thanks, thought Ralphie. *What's your name? I sure as hell don't remember, but you know what? I haven't seen you for years.*

For the next minute or so, Ralphie blacked out.

When he woke up, he was sitting on a picnic bench. He looked up. Leaves had fallen like splats of paint onto the neighboring basketball court. No one was playing basketball.

"Okay, Ralphie, you can throw up now," said the big man. "If you want."

"Who are you?"

"You know me, Ralphie. We're from back home. We came to find you," said the Big Man.

"And this guy here...you know him for sure. That's Vinnie. Say hi, Vinnie."

"Hi," said Vinnie.

Ralphie didn't throw up. But he wasn't happy.

"No. I'm okay. I don't need to throw up."

"Good. That's good, Ralphie. So we're sitting in a park. On a bench. It's right by your restaurant. Nice place. And a blessing to good food in the Northwest of our great country. Vinnie and I had some ordered in last night. Yeah. Good."

Stuff was swimming around Ralphie, but it was all slowly coalescing into total horror.

"You guys gonna kill me?" he said softly.

"Hey, Vinnie. He's awake. So why should we kill you?"

"I'm on a contract, right? A hit."

"Hmm. Vinnie, am I a hitman?"

"I'm not really sure," said Vinnie.

The big man took out a huge gun, the kind of handgun that could blow a hole the size of a fist through Ralphie's chest. He put it on the picnic table.

"Hmm. Well, you be the judge, huh?" said the big man.

Ralphie found there were tears in his eyes. "You guys don't understand. I'm sorry. I really am. What was I supposed to do? Jesus. What the hell was I supposed to do? I couldn't pay what I owed."

The big man said, "Ralphie. You got an operation here. Looks good. Maybe we'll kill you and collect from your widow. But you know what? Vinnie here, Vinnie says you might have a stash. Shit, that would go a long way with the boss. We give him some money, he's happier. What do you think?"

At first, in the first flurry of that big fist and the confusion, in his heart of hearts, Ralphie though he was dead. But now, he wasn't dead. He was feeling better. His breaths were coming easier. And this big man here…This big man was actually smiling.

"Why would Vinnie think I have a stash?" Ralphie said. "Vinnie hasn't been around."

The big man shrugged. He clicked off the safety of his gun. He grabbed Ralphie's mouth and stuck it between his teeth.

"I was in a good mood. I'm getting into a bad mood."

Ralphie felt his bowels go loose.

He peed himself.

He thought fast.

Phil! Phil could bail him out.

"Yeah. Shit. I got a stash. I got a friend whose giving me some money today. We can go now if you want. He's expecting me."

The big man said, "If this is bullshit, you are dead. Your friend is dead. And Vinnie here." He showed a great big smile of teeth, including a gold cap. "Vinnie gets your wife."

Ralphie nodded. "Take me. I'll bring you there. Phil will pay. Phil's a good guy."

They walked him back to a car and the big man sat with him in the back seat.

He told them how to get to Phil Roman's house.

28

Phil Roman sat in front of a small-screen TV. Beside him was a huge package of cashews. He grabbed a handful. He crunched them. He watched some more of his DVD from his most recent free, mail-order "trial". It was disk three of the third season of *Gilmore Girls*. Good stuff.

Phil normally didn't subscribe to any service for very long. What he did was to let his memberships lapse until the companies tried to entice him back with free downloads and extended trials. It wasn't that he couldn't afford them, but old habits die hard.

He was halfway through the episode when his good friend Adam Even came out of the back of the home, where he'd recently moved in.

"Oh, yeah," he said. "This is a great show."

"Yep. Very clever dialogue."

They watched together for a few minutes.

"Really appreciate you letting me stay, Phil."

Phil laughed. "No problem. That's the stripper's room. No strippers are visiting me now, so you get it. And you know what? You do not have to strip."

"Thanks."

"You doin' okay? I offered you that TV."

"No. I'm fine. Mostly reading. Just need to get away. That or go to see a shrink."

Phil shuddered. "No. Do not do that!"

"Anyway, I brought my laptop and I knew you don't have Wi-Fi here…"

Phil grinned in self-satisfaction. "I do my email at the library. It's free there."

"Oh, yeah. That's smart. No, what I was saying was that I've got a portable Wi-Fi thing so me and my laptop... we're just fine."

"Look, we're buddies! You help me, I help you. Glad to have you here."

"Thanks."

"One thing. Do you talk to yourself?"

"Sometimes. I guess I do," said Adam Even.

Phil gave a hearty laugh. "Good. Glad I'm not the only nut in this town. Yeah, I heard you last night. Sounds like you do a good Scots accent."

"Och. When the wind blows twixt the trees and the heather and the spirit is on me sporran."

Phil laughed.

"Okay. So thanks again. I'm going out for a bit to get some stuff. Need anything?"

"No, I'm fine."

"Okay." Adam jingled his keys in his jacket pocket. "See you later."

"Yeah. Say, you wanna watch some of this Flash Gordon serial I got in my latest 'deal'?"

"Sure. Why not."

Adam went out and got into his Saab and drove away.

Phil went back to watching *Gilmore Girls*.

By the time they got to Phil Roman's house, Ralphie was starting to feel like he had a chance. They weren't gonna kill him. Bang him up a bit. And get some money from him. Only thing was, he didn't have money. He was counting on Phil to save his ass.

"What's this about a vault?" said Vinnie.

"I'm telling you, this guy's an eccentric. He says the timer on his vault goes off this afternoon and he's gonna let me have some money."

"The money is all we care about, Ralphie," said the big man. On the short ride, Ralphie had learned he was called Chomp.

"Sounds like you can get us some. Enough to hold off the uh… old whack job, know what I mean?"

Yeah… Ralphie knew what he meant.

They'd stopped off at a gas station, filled up. They did something else, but Ralphie wasn't sure what.

He was just sitting in the back seat alongside Vinnie, trying to recover his wits.

"Okay, so you go first. You introduce us as investors, see? We're looking at…what are they called, Vinnie?"

"Franchises."

"Yeah. Franchises. Bringing pizza and enlightenment to the Wild West. Sounds good to me. Sounds like somethin' I could get behind. Right now, though, we need some hard cold cash or you're gonna get a hard cold gun up your ass. Capiche?"

"I understand. Sure. I'm real sorry. I didn't know what else to do."

"Look. It's all business, right? And I hope…" said Chomp. "I sincerely hope that everyone comes out of this smilin'. Meanwhile…" He shrugged his big shoulders and it looked like one of those rolling earthquakes they had down in L.A.

The house was off River Road. It was a squat little ranch that needed paint, bad.

"What, this is it? This guy is rich?"

"He's a miser. What can I say?"

"Whatever. So he's expecting you about now?"

"Yes. That is what I said."

Chomp pulled up. They got out and walked up the weed-ridden, cracked sidewalk.

"Yard could use a mowing, that's for sure," said Chomp. "Okay, Ralphie. Go up and knock on the door. We're right behind you, okay?"

"I hear you."

Ralphie went up to the door. To get to Phil's door you had to climb some steps, slimy with wet moss. Moss was everywhere on Phil's house, especially the roof, where it clung like an alien seepage from the skies.

Ralphie allowed himself a deep breath and he rallied. He brought together in himself everything he knew about sales and projecting personality. Then he knocked on the door.

"Open!" boomed a voice.

"Uh…it's Ralphie."

"Of course it's Ralphie. You got my pie?"

"Sure. Gotta talk to you first. Could you open the door?"

The voice got louder and more annoyed. "I said the door is open. Come on in."

He looked back at Chomp. Chomp seemed baffled but still in a shrugging mode. He pointed and made a turning motion and mouthed "Get the fuck in and we'll come after you."

"Okay," said Ralphie.

He pushed open the door and walked in.

Phil was parked in his big high-backed chair, legs up on an ottoman, TV controls by one elbow, books and comics by the other, looking mighty pleased with himself.

Mighty fat and happy. To one side he had a huge plastic container of Costco cashews. He was chewing some now.

"Hey, Phil. Thanks for having me over, dude. I brought along some friends who want to invest in the restaurant and stuff. Like we talked about."

"They got money?" said Phil, looking unconcerned. Still he reached over to the controls and hit the pause button.

"Well, they're gonna talk about that in a minute."

He moved ahead into the hall. To either side of him were bulging bookshelves, stocked to the brim with magazines, comics, books, pamphlets, old books, new books, and boxes of newsletters of some sort. That was the story of Phil's entire house. It was stuffed and stuffed once more and then again with more paper—some new, but most very old.

"So who are your buddies?"

"They're guys from back home, Phil. This is Vinnie. This is Chomp."

They came in, Vinnie and Chomp did, and they closed the door behind them.

Phil took one look at them and his self-satisfied smile left his face.

"Oh, hello," he said. He stopped eating his cashews.

"Hello," said Vinnie.

"Hello," said Chomp. "Ralphie, you didn't tell Mr. Bowman here…"

"Roman," said Phil.

"You didn't tell Mr. Bowman here what you're here for," said Chomp.

"So, Phil," said Ralphie. "You were expecting me, right?"

"Uh, yeah."

"You got the money?"

"Yes. But what does…"

"I need it."

Phil was frowning now. He looked over to the side of his lounge chair, found an envelope.

He struggled his close to 400 pounds up and waddled over to Ralphie.

"That's what I can do, Ralph."

He gave the envelope to Ralphie. Immediately Chomp reached out with a long arm and grabbed the envelope out of Ralphie's hand. He ripped it open.

Took a quick look. "What the fuck, Ralphie? I see five hundred bucks, max."

"Look. I don't know who you are but you have no right to—"

Chomp stepped forward and gave a gentle shove. Phil stumbled back as though he'd been hit by a truck. He tripped over the ottoman and fell back into his lounge chair. A pile of mail and magazines fell over into his lap.

Vinnie said, "Ralphie, you've been lying to us."

"I ain't been lyin'…" He turned desperately to Phil. "Phil, you gotta stay with me here. You got to have to know I'd need more than this to do Vegas."

"Oh, Vegas. I see," said Chomp. He stuck the money into his pocket. "But Ralphie, you mentioned that this fat ass has money here. Like a vault. What time does it open?"

Phil Roman looked like a big fish for the first time pulled out of a happy ocean of fun and landed onto a shoreline of big trouble. His big mouth was opening and closing, and he seemed to be struggling to breathe. "Vault?"

"Yeah, dude. You told me you got plenty of money here. And you mentioned a vault," said Ralphie.

"That's a Jack Benny joke."

"Jack Benny?" said Chomp. "Who the fuck is this Jack Benny?"

Vinnie said, "Hell if I know."

Ralphie said, "But you got money stashed here. Look, I'm in big trouble. It's all gonna be okay and it will come out in the wash, I swear it, Phil. But what I need now is a lot more cash than this!"

"Do you hear what I'm saying to you, you fat asshole? You've got money here. Stashed. Ralphie says so and you know what? I can smell it." For some reason, Chomp was incensed. He obviously hadn't taken much of a shine to Phil Roman.

"I meant…what I'm saying…what I said," gulped Phil, looking not only as though he was not only on the verge of a heart attack but had just shit himself, "was that I've got value here."

"Where?"

"My… my stuff. My books, my pulps… look mister. I'm outta of my league here. I was just helping Ralph out with his restaurant."

"He says you want to fuck his wife."

Phil Roman was taken aback. He shook his head. "Can't do that. I'm a bit…uhm…well… impotent you know. I do appreciate it. But…"

"Get the hell away from that phone!"

Chomp stomped over and knocked the landline phone—an old thing—off the counter by Phil. He took the cord and yanked it out of the wall.

"Fat asshole. You met Ralphie. You met his wife," he said. He pulled out his gun. "You eat Jersey stuff, but I hear you prefer Chicago crap. But who do you think you are dealing with when you deal with Ralphie and his twat? Sweetheart amateurs? What's the matter with you?"

Phil Roman did his fish-gulping motions again.

"Yeah, right. And I hear from Ralphie you like crime fiction. So Ralphie comes along, you don't recognize a Jersey con man?"

Phil Roman was white. He seemed to have a hard time even gulping.

"I'm sick of your fat ass already," said Chomp. "Vinnie go out and get the can."

"Okay."

"I know there's gotta be some cash around here, and I want it. Fat boy here is a cash person. I can tell. Probably waves cash in front of dying old ladies to get their book collections."

Phil was as pale as a fish belly.

Vinnie was back. He had a metal can with him.

"Right. Cash. I want some cash, right now, fat boy. I know it's here. You have it somewhere, right? I know your kind. You worms live in little hovels in Jersey City and Brooklyn and your apartments smell like cabbage. Hmm?"

Vinnie said, "I think you might be right."

Chomp took out a large butane lighter. With a flick the light was on. A flame, blue and deadly, danced with a fairy excitement about the green and purple plastic and metal.

"Okay, Vinnie. Just splash a little of that stuff over by the Fucked Up Tales, will you?"

Vinnie did that. It came out in gushes and spilled on the wood in front of the bookshelf shrine.

"Cash, fat boy. I want some cash."

Chomp held the flame under a shelf of Mylar-encased pulps. It sparked. The flames licked up the old pulp paper, hungry and eager.

"Noooooooooo!" screamed Phil Roman. Without warning the large book collector stood up and lunged toward the killer.

"What the hell," said Chomp. He sidestepped the lunge and tripped over a pile of books.

The burning pulps flopped over into the spill of gasoline that Vinnie had provided.

Greedy flames reached up for a stack of old *Weird Tales*.

"Noooo!" Phil screamed again. This time, though, Phil Roman did not charge anyone. He went suddenly rigid, clutched his chest and gasped. He staggered about for a moment like a giant bull in a small china shop, and then he stumbled forward into a huge, ungainly, and poorly planned bookshelf which obliged by toppling over directly on top of him, leaving him buried in a grave of heavy books.

There was no more sound from Phil Roman.

For a moment, Vinnie and Ralphie stared in horror at the holocaust that Chomp had caused. Just a tuft of dyed black hair could be seen of Phil Roman, poking out from his pile of precious books.

The fire on the *Weird Tales* leapt up, like Hell's own judgment. It spread out over *Horror Stories, Terror Tales, Dime Mystery* and into a whole area of rare and more valuable pulp magazines.

"Asshole," screamed Chomp. "Fat freakin' asshole!" He got up and surveyed the situation. "Well, shit. We gotta sign off. Grab Ralphie, Vince. Don't let him run. He's still prime meat."

Chomp pulled out his gun. "We better make sure we finish this job, just in case." He stepped forward carefully over piles of strewn books and put the business end of his gun against the black of Phil Roman's hair. "Fat assho—"

A sudden wind swept out from the hallway. It swarmed around them, fanning the flames, but not dowsing them.

In the hallway the intruders could make out a figure, stepping through the smoke and the fumes.

"You've woken me up! There's the Devil to pay for that! Aye, and what is this? Fire? And why was I not summoned to join in on the fun?"

"Fuck me," said Chomp.

Coming toward them was a dwarf. It hobbled. It went back and forth, back and forth as it walked. It wore what looked like heavy, lead boots. On its head was a cap. And the cap was not only red, but dripping with red as though recently stuck into a can of crimson paint.

Chomp had been in this business long enough to sense danger. And this was it.

He focused.

He felt better. He was on point. Adrenalin had kicked in. He was a pro, and he'd been trained as a kid and in the army. If there was any guy in East Passaic who knew how to aim and point and fire a hand held weapon, it was Earl K. Chompski.

He squeezed the trigger.

Once.

Twice.

The bullets were monsters. And they landed right where he'd aimed them. Straight into this dwarf's chest.

They blew him back.

Once.

Twice.

But that dwarf didn't fall. In fact, he started to bob back and forth and actually grinned. The flames sent shadows dancing up the wall behind him, and glimmers of something not quite like skin glinted beneath glowing eyes.

With a flurry of sparks and a gust of wind that came out of nowhere—the dwarf expanded.

"Ooooooh," he said. "Ooooh."

He started forward, and suddenly he *was* the flames and the wind that were consuming the books.

"I see with my little eye… a tiny leetle wee human. Oooh, I like you."

With the voice of a hurricane, surrounded in fire and smoke, the thing rushed forward, skirting around what was left of Ralphie. As it drew closer to Chomp and Vinnie, its claws extended.

"Ooooooh. Ooooh. Delicious. Tasty. I like your Mr. Ralphie."

Vinnie and Chomp watched, stunned as the claws that had once been smoke and fire were thrust in from the back and through Ralphie's chest. Blood spurted, but not enough to kill the flames eating up the pulp collection.

What Ralphie saw was Satan himself looking up from Hell.

"Why, good day, Ralph. We are so happy to welcome you. But ooops. Wait. Looks as though there are things you must do first. Well, tra la la and hidey ho. It's off to work we go."

And the dwarf of fire and wind simply penetrated the rest of Ralphie. Blood burst everywhere. Suddenly, Ralphie's hands were no longer hands but huge claws and Ralphie's teeth were no longer just teeth but huge fangs.

And Ralphie, not a big man, was growing.

Growing and growing, eyes red and eager.

Blood leaked out from his ears as something else poked out from the lobes.

Pointy ears.

His nose grew, large and peculiar, with tufts of rough hair that stuck out, like patches of rough on a golf course.

And his eyes. His eyes simply popped out, both of them. They rolled along the ratty rug, trailing veins, and torn muscles and gore. From what should have been empty pits, new eyes glared out, leering at their prey.

The chest grew big—werewolf big.

"Fuck!" said Chomp and he simply unloaded the rest of his magazine into that growing, swelling chest.

Vinnie pulled out his gun as well. He started firing. But he was the closest to the creature.

A claw picked him from under his neck and held him. The thing sniffed him like a wolf sniffs a prospective dinner.

"Oh my, dear lads," said Robin Redcap. "I have a treat this afternoon!"

29

"I dunno," Lynn said. "He just wasn't there."

"So what did you do?"

"I just closed up. I came in, Ralphie wasn't there but stuff was cooking. I had this weird feeling, so I got the stuff outta the oven and put it in the fridge. Then I closed the place up and came home. After that, I start to really worry. I wait around. I call his cell. Nothing. I call his cell again. Nothing. Nothing, nothing nothing."

"You think he ran off with some woman?" asked her lover. There was hope in his voice.

"Ralphie? No fuckin' way. He was supposed to go over to Phil Roman's and pick up some money for Las Vegas. You remember that, Jack, don't you?"

"Oh, sorry. Right."

She was sitting at the apartment's kitchen table now. There was a big glass of red wine in front of her. She was sipping from it. She held her cell phone close to her ear, as though somehow the feel of plastic was a comfort. The man on the other end was her "side" game—her distraction. She wasn't sure distraction was what she needed, but she felt very alone.

"So I'm calling you."

"I'm glad you did. I didn't think I'd hear from you until next week when you got back."

"Oh, honey baby, I miss you. I don't really want to go."

"I know."

"Honey baby, you're my guy. You know that."

There was a silence at the other end of the cell phone line.

"You there?" she said.

"I'm…well… I'm overwhelmed."

"Overwhelmed. You and your college graduate student big words. Don't stop. I love 'em."

"You can still go to college. When we get away from Ralph. We'll do that, okay? I'll be teaching at a great paying place and you can go back to school. You've got plenty of credits, I know."

"I do. Ralphie… he kept me back."

"I'll be at a good university. A professor. Next year. Rutgers and Princeton and Stanford. They're all interested. And I'll take care of you. No more pizza, honey baby. You go back to school, you learn what you want. Have a career. Or not. We can make babies if you like."

Her breath caught in her throat. She'd go off birth control and pop out a kid or two, and he'd be happy. They'd be gorgeous kids too. You bet.

"Well, honey baby, we have to talk about that. But right now, all I've got is in that restaurant and food cart. And all I got is caught up in Ralphie. And he's not here."

"I could come over."

"Bad idea. Very bad idea," she sighed. "I shouldn't have called. I'm sorry. It's just that… I don't know, I've got this weird feeling."

"I'm just here at my place, studying for my orals next week. You know you can call me whenever. But let's hang up now. If Ralphie hasn't shown up in a half hour, call me back. Okay?

"Yeah. Yeah, I guess you're right." She banged a fist against the table. "Oh, I wish you were here to hold me. Just for a few seconds."

"I am there, honey baby," said her lover. "I'm there in your heart, just like you are here in mine."

She'd met Ted last year. He'd come every Tuesday and Thursday for a couple of slices and a soda. They'd started talking, and it wasn't long before she was sneaking out nights to see him.

Gonna see some girlfriends, Ralphie.

Ladies' stuff.

Ted wasn't just a wonderful and thoughtful lover. They could talk about things. He was going for a doctorate in World Literature and he read a lot. He gave her books to read, and they talked about the books.

She didn't know what the heck she was going to do about Ralphie.

The restaurant was going okay, but now she had some kind of hope. He was in love with her, Ted was. He said when he got a job at some other university he'd steal her from Ralphie.

Now, though, there was some kind of trouble brewing. She felt it deep in her bones.

"Look," said Ted. "I've got to read a bit more but I'll text you to check in. And if something serious happened, which I doubt, you know you can call me."

"Yeah. Yeah, okay."

"I love you, honey baby."

"I love you, too…"

She went into the family room, sat on the couch, and continued to sip her wine. There was nothing she could do but wait for Ralphie, and hope that the sick feeling growing in the pit of her stomach was just indigestion.

It was November in Eugene, Oregon. Cold and damp had moved back in.

Cold, damp, and dark. She didn't like it here, not really, not the way the clouds got so low. Dark and dark and darker, they hung onto the buttes and wisps of misty dark reached down as though to snatch up creatures and lift them up to dark and hungry maws.

Now, as she sat and sipped wine and watched a cop show on TV, a wind had started, spattering a breath of rain against the window pane. A tree branch, naked of leaves, clicked against the cheap glass.

Click click.

Click click click.

Lynn shivered and drew her Snuggie tighter around her. She

downed her wine and poured another glass.

Then she fired up another Camel.

"Camels, huh?" she remembered Ralphie saying after their first few dates.

"Yeah? So what?"

"Nothing. Just shows…you like humps."

She'd laughed then. She'd always liked him. He was fun. And say what you liked about Ralphie, he had dreams. He had ambitions. Most of it was crap, but that was life.

Halfway through the Camel and a quarter through the glass of wine, footsteps slushed and slurred up the outside steps. They were on the second floor of a cheap set of apartments not far from the restaurant. The steps hesitated… and then they continued.

Thump. Thump. Thump.

The steps hushed and thumped along the landing and then stopped outside the door.

A key fumbled at the lock and a hand wrestled with the door.

"Ralphie?" she said. "Is that you?"

There was no response. No rattling of the door, no trying of the lock.

Just silence.

"What the fuck?" she said. She reached over to the remote control. Clicked off the TV. "Ralphie? Ralphie, is that you?"

Shit. Maybe it was Ted. Maybe he had gotten worried about her. Maybe he'd come over.

But there was just silence now. Only the silence gave way to a renewed clicking of those skeleton claws on the cheap window panes. A gush of wind. And she could almost feel the low clouds, reach wispy arms down…

Down.

Down.

Down.

"Screw this," she said.

She had a .38-caliber handgun she kept underneath the coffee table.

It was a nice shiny one, too. Ralphie was a gun nut. He had plenty of guns. He naturally wanted his wife to have a nice one too.

She got it out. Took the safety off.

The lock rattled.

"Let me in," said a voice like something belching up from an ancient grave. "Let me in."

She remembered this story she'd had to read in high school. It was called "The Monkey's Paw."

In the story a woman's son gets mangled in a factory accident but the woman had a special severed monkey's paw some gypsy had given her. One wish. One special wish.

And she wanted her son back.

Thing was, of course, the horror on the other side of THAT door? Uh uh. Nope. Not THAT back.

She had that same kind of feeling now.

"I'm calling the cops, right now, whoever you are."

She reached for the cell phone, but before she could grab it, the door rattled again. And something bowed it in. It was like the door in that Shirley Jackson movie about the haunted house.

But this door wasn't like the door in the movie. It was cheap, and it didn't hold.

It burst open.

The thing on the other side dripped. Stuff hung from its face and arms like wisps, like little tentacles.

It dripped blood.

And then, step by step, in boots made of metal, it shuffled forward.

"Honey baby," it rasped. "Ralphie's home!"

30

"**G**ood evening, Adam!" said Robin Redcap. The goblin had some pliers and was prying .38-caliber bullets from his vest. "Well, now. Back home again, eh?"

"Nowhere else to go," said Adam Even. He sat at his desk in his study. On the desk was his crate, and in the crate, open now, was his noose.

"I thought you might show up here," the creature said. It was—different.

Although it was still most certainly a dwarf, it seemed to own other dimensions now than mere height and weight. It sparkled with an evil luster, like diamonds in a dragon's horde.

"I must say, I had no idea that this day would give me such a boost. Such a treat. Why look at my cap!" The goblin reached up with one hand and rubbed his hat. He pulled away a red hand and droplets of blood rolled down and slid over its cheeks like thick red tears.

He tasted it. He looked, Adam thought, like a fat little boy enjoying a nice sugar cone of delicious, special ice cream.

"Yes, my dear, wee boy. No need for birds and squirrels or the odd stray dog or cat this day."

"I see."

"Well, I have to say," said Robin Redcap. He paused for a moment, looked in a mirror and with that mirror's help removed a bullet stuck in a cheek. "I'm sorry. I was hoping that when my dear associate showed up, you'd get to meet her. Alas, she is busy. It's been a busy day for all, and there is work yet to do. We must finish and be on our way."

The creature's eyes were strong and wide and, like the cap on his head, blood dripped from their corners, as if its head had sprung a leak. The thing's teeth, which had once seemed yellow with age, were larger, and they glittered like sharpened crystals.

"Whatever you say, Robbie," Adam replied. "All I have to say is that I'm glad it will be over."

"Och. No fear of the One Down Under, eh? No fear of the Prince of Darkness? I understand that Our Lord enjoys the odd comedian once in a while. And my, what can I say? You *are* odd."

"That is true."

"Hmm." The goblin pulled out the bullet and tossed it away contemptuously. "Well, I'll leave you to your noose. You know what you must do. I have other business to attend to this night. And then it's off to other wonderful mischief. Oh, and the plans…the plans. Well then, must get on with things, mustn't we." The goblin stood and got the noose out of the box. With ease and skill, he threw it up over a rafter. The ceiling tiles had been removed and the insulation torn free, in preparation for this moment. Satisfied, the creature placed a chair beneath the rope, tied off the rope supporting the noose just so, and tested it.

"That's right. This will do nicely."

"Good," Adam said dully. He rose and moved toward the chair.

"I have to thank you, Robin Redcap. You are allowing me to die at home, and by my own hand. We've talked about this before and you know that I've begged and begged for you to just let me get on with it. When I got back from the store and found my friend's house in flames, I knew what must have happened.

"It was my fault. I should never have gone there, never taken the noose out of this house. My friend had nothing to do with this, and I killed him."

Adam climbed onto the chair. He put it over his head and dropped it around his neck. It was a good fit. "Just pull it up a bit, would you? I'm ready to go."

Suddenly a cell phone ringtone sounded.

Robin Redcap pulled out an iPhone. The image was surreal, and somehow very, very funny. "Yes?" He listened for a moment. "Excellent. I'm on my way."

"You can stick around?" said Adam Even.

"To suck up your measly energy? Sorry. Other fish to fry, old sir. Other fish to fry."

And just like that, Robin Redcap left. It was a whisking departure, a flash of rainbow tinged light and power.

Adam Even stood very still on the chair and prepared himself.

He knew what was next. It was only nothing. Nothing nothing nothing.

Just like his life.

31

"**S**o, why are we here?" said Madrigal Harper. She ushered Skylar through the door that Natosha held open for them. He brightened noticeably.

"Hi, Nat."

"Hi, Sky."

Natosha shook her head. "My parents! They just went away. They said, 'Girl you're almost eighteen. You'll be fine on your own.'" She sighed. "And I'm sorry. I know I act like I'm such a haughty Goth and all, but I don't know. I'm kind of freaked out, after all that's been going on, and those noises over at Mr. Even's house."

Bill Edmonds, who'd followed Maddy in, nodded. It was late, and the day had been total hell. Maddy had brought out a bottle of Jim Beam and cracked it open. He felt a little better now, but he'd brought the whiskey with him, just in case.

"I am so glad you're here," said Natosha. She wasn't wearing any dark makeup tonight. She just looked like a normal teen in sweater and jeans. "I was okay, but then I turned on the news. I heard about the man's house that burned down, and I remembered that Mr. Even mentioned he had a friend who sold books. I started thinking about those sounds—his cats?"

She shivered.

Maddy watched in amazement as Sky, who could barely be coaxed into a hug for his family, walked over and put an arm around Natosha. "Nat. The good news is that Mr. Bullfinch is going to be fine. And we have a new friend here to help us with these ghosts; I think I hear her car outside now."

The woman who came to the door wasn't pretty, Maddy thought, but she was handsome. It was a term she'd heard used over the years, but never really understood until that moment. She was dressed sensibly, in boots, dark pants, and a jacket that might, or might not be covering any number of things. The woman carried a couple of large jugs of clear liquid.

"Hi," said Natosha. "I like your cross. It's huge! And so... silvery."

"That's because it is. My name is Isabella, and this cross..." She reached down and lifted it slowly, bringing it to her lips, "was blessed by the Holy Father Himself."

"The Holy Father?"

"That would be the pope, dear," said Maddy. "The one and only."

Natosha nodded. Her eyes widened, just a little, and fixed on the glittering pendant.

"I'm thinking after all this is over, I'm going to start going to church."

"Don't let the danger of a moment, or the evil of a night, make such a decision for you," Isabella said gravely. "If there is a church that is meant for you—it will find you."

"So, Maddy," Bill said, changing the subject, "you want to fill us in on what you found out about the nooses? You said it was important..."

Maddy nodded. She pulled out a small notebook from her hip pocket, flipped it open, and after a moment, began to speak.

"I've been working with another friend of Bullfinch's, a man named Mack. He has incredible Internet skills, and between us, we've managed to find some information I wish we'd had much sooner. It looks like there's a single person who is the focus of the suicides, but it's still a little confusing."

"How so?"

"Well, it revolves around a real estate company. You may remember a few years ago, that whole market fell apart here."

"And all over the country."

"Well, prices went down for houses. Fewer folks were buying. But there was this one company that did well. And you know what?"

"I'm starting to get an idea. I'm betting I'll recognize some addresses."

"You're a smart man. Yes, all these houses with the nooses were sold by the same company."

"And more than that. For a while, they had a little helper."

"A little helper?"

"Yes. Here, I have a picture." She brought out a small manila envelope from a pocket.

In it was a small photo. She showed it to Bill.

"It's just a little old lady," he said.

"Well, that little old lady helped sell some houses. And all the house she sold—including the old Eugene Hotel, ghost and all—contained boxes with those old nooses."

"And so," said Skylar, "the new owners started finding them."

"I guess we know what happened next," Natosha said. "The Noose Club."

Bill Edmonds shook his head. "I still don't get it. What's the point? Old nooses. Ghosts. What the hell did Bullfinch say... goblins? What's the point?"

"We can sort that out later," said Maddy. "Who is this woman?"

Maddy carried the picture over to Isabella. "What do you think? Bullfinch tells me you're the one who figured out we're up against goblins. Any idea who this woman might be?"

Maddy handed Isabella the picture.

Isabella stared at the picture closely. She blinked. She crossed herself.

"I know this one. I have followed her before, but never been this close. I believe you will find that she is working with the other one. Both of them are very dangerous."

"You don't have to tell us about the one," Bill cut in. "That thing on the roof..."

Isabella Ferrara tapped the picture. "It is Alison Gross."

"Alison Gross? What the hell are you talking about? Who is Alison Gross? You say that as if we should know..." said Bill Nichols.

"There is a song," Isabella said, almost wistfully. "It is a very old folk song but the group, the English group, Steeleye Span. They do a wonderful version. 'Alison Gross,' she sang. 'She must be...the ugliest witch in the North Country'."

"Oh, great," said Bill Edmonds. "Now we've got ghosts, goblins, *and* witches!"

"She is no witch," said Isabella. "That is what the song says, but there are older versions—truer. She's a female goblin. She disguises herself as an old woman, or a witch."

"Why?"

"Wait a minute," said Natosha. "Okay. So actually, believe it or not, you're making some sense here."

They all turned and stared.

"I have very good Internet skills and I've been researching a lot," said Natosha. "And Sky here, he's been helping. He's good at it too."

"At first we researched ghosts. But even poltergeists don't wreak the kind of havoc we've been having here in Eugene," said Sky. "These fairies—fairies aren't just cute little Tinkerbells— are... like everything that has plagued human beings since who knows when. But not in cities. Out in the country, out where there's darkness and mystery. Know what I mean?"

"Fuck the fairies," Bill cut in. "I know what I saw. I shot a monster!"

"Fairie is a—state of being," Isabella said. "I have dealt with her monsters, big and small. Still, they are fairies, and these—the ones who have brought death to your city—are big ones. Goblins, ghosts, fairies, call them whatever you want."

"I am absolutely sure of one thing," Bill said. "I have no idea what the hell you are talking about."

"You are a brave man and you saved my friend," said Isabella.

"But your experience limits you. I have been fighting this particular war for a very long time. You would do well to trust your fear, and your eyes. Your experience is almost certain to fail you."

"Fair enough," Bill said. "I know we're dealing with something fast, powerful, hard to kill—and that does not like holy water. Also, it wants something, but damned if I can figure out what."

That's when the lights went out.

Mack Macklemore stopped the rental car. He got out and went to the bench at the edge of the square park. A lonesome street lamp hung above the dead grass like Charon's boat lamp.

He shivered and opened up his laptop.

He needed a few moments away from the wheel to check his various networks and connections. He knew time was precious, but it was more than just a responsibility to him. The network they called O.C.L.T. was his life, and he couldn't concentrate on the job at hand without being certain he wasn't missing something—some bit of data newly discovered, something he'd overlooked.

He logged in and leaned closer to the screen, shutting out his surroundings as he immersed himself in multiple streams of data, and a host of email and text accounts.

He was suddenly aware of an odd sensation. There was a prickling at the back of his neck. Then he glanced up, suddenly aware that he was not alone.

It was an old squat woman in an expensive coat. Her straggly gray and knotty hair grew out the side of a floppy hat like bat's wings. Mack thought of the photos he'd passed on to Maddy, and his throat grew dry.

"Good evening, kind sir," she said in a scratchy English accent. "Might an ailing old biddy sit for a moment on your bench?"

32

Maddy screamed despite herself.

"Stay still. Stay where you are," said Isabella. "Whatever you do, don't move."

An impossible wind moved around the house, like a huskily breathing wolf in search of prey. Streetlights glimmered, but then seemed suddenly covered by a cloak of damp mist. There was a wet, musty scent in the air—like that of an old dog just in from the rain.

The door blew open. A figured scurried and scampered in, and then, before they could track its progress, it was gone.

The lights flickered dimly, but did not come fully back to life.

"You see anything?" said Bill. He had his gun out.

Maddy had her gun out as well. "No."

"You'll be lookin' for me then, my laddies and lasses. Well, I be here. I come in with the night, but I leave with the dead."

The voice was ambient. It seemed to come from everywhere and nowhere.

"And then ye'll be askin' yourselves, who is this? Who comes in from the glen and the heather? Why, 'tis only a wee bit of trouble—a passing curse. I'll be gone soon. Gone when I've got what I've come for."

"It's him," Isabella hissed.

There was a rustling, a flurry of motion—and then the sound of a rope sliding over wood. The ceilings were vaulted, and the rough wooden beams were open and accessible. Everyone turned, drawn to the sound. The length of ancient hemp seemed, almost, to sparkle, rising in slow motion, cresting the dark beam and slipping over the other side. It stopped with a jerk that set it swinging five feet from the floor.

At its end...

A noose.

"So, you wish to know why the nooses, then," said the voice of the invisible presence. "Perhaps there is no reason? Perhaps it's simply a joke? You know, my kind, my people, we love to be a nuisance... get it?"

An evil chuckle, a sound so chilling it dropped the temperature in the room, reverberated from the walls.

Cursing, Bill gauged the sound, put together what he'd seen of the thing's movements, and opened fire.

A mirror shattered.

"Bad luck! Seven years' worth, eh?"

The gun was knocked from Bill's hand. He tried to leap forward and grapple with the flickering shadow that passed his gaze, but he could not. He was paralyzed.

"I can't move!" Maddy screamed. "Natosha! Sky! Get out! Isabella, do something!"

"You may try," the voice whispered, the sound somehow carrying and seeming to blow on fetid breath into each of their ears. "'Tis the goblin's blessing, straight from the bubbling cauldron. A powerful bit of magic. I use it rarely, but then tonight is a rare night. You'll not be moving just yet."

Isabella fell over, gasping. She tried to reach for the bottles she'd carried in, but she found herself unable to move. It was as though someone had rammed dozens of icicles through her body. She tasted the tang of old magic, and cursed herself inwardly for not warding herself, and the home, immediately.

"So," said the voice, "I only ask for one more thing, and then I shall take my leave from this dreary place. I have supped well and grown powerful beyond my expectations, and I thank you all for the entertainment. You are all insignificant, but one. I have sensed him, several times. Why, there he is! Young Master Skylar?"

"I can't move," said Sky.

"Don't you touch my son!" howled Maddy.

"Sky," said Natosha. "Start praying. In Jesus Christ's name, I rebuke you foul spirit of a night and…"

With a snarl and a flash of power, Natosha was knocked off her feet, landing in a heap, blood leaking from her mouth.

"Skylar. You are now mine!" said the voice.

Slowly, as if he'd been lifted physically, Skylar rose from the floor. He was still paralyzed, and the others watched in horror as he floated slowly, almost lazily, toward the dangling noose.

"Like threading a needle!"

The noose slipped around Sky's neck.

"No, you fucking bastard! No!" screamed Bill Edmonds.

"I am sorry. I am sure Mother Madrigal—such a sweet name—that you would give yourself in place of your son. Sadly, it simply would not be the same. You see, there is a magic in young Skylar, and I need it to possess the full power that I deserve. There is nothing like a good hanging to squeeze out what is mine."

The rope grew taut.

The noose began to tighten.

And it tightened around Skylar's neck.

Maddy could not deal with the reality of what she was seeing, so she drifted into memory. She remembered when Sky had been four years old. They were walking outside one day in the middle of summer. The sky had been very clear.

"Mommy, look, a falling star!"

"Yes, Sky. Yes, isn't it beautiful?"

"Mommy, I wished for something. Like I heard you could. Mommy, did you wish for something?"

"Why yes, Sky. I did."

His eyes were bright. "Something good?"

"Well, yes."

"So what did you wish for?"

"That would be telling."

"Oh please, Mommy. Something for me?"

"Yes. Yes, of course, Sky."

"What is it, Mommy? What is it?"

"Okay. I just wished that you would be happy, Sky."

Sky stopped on the sidewalk. "Mom!" he said, stamping his little foot with frustration. "I am happy! What I need is a cool train set!"

The rope tightened with a creak and she snapped back to the present.

The noose around her son's neck had tightened.

He struggled. Somehow he struggled and broke his paralysis. He reached up and put his hands around the rope. He pulled.

"Oh, my." It was a cackle more than anything else. "Oh, dear! The fish on the fishing pole! He is a strong one. See how he struggles."

The rope tightened. It pulled up. Up and up and up. And although Sky held on and took some of the weight off his neck by his grip on the rope, it was clear that it was too much for him. As if some invisible crane was slowly hauling him up, he rose, and whatever force had been lifting him began to seep away.

Madrigal Harper stared in horror as her son hung before her, eyes large, dying.

33

Mack was a no-nonsense kind of guy, and he didn't believe in beating around the bush.

"You're Alison Gross, right?"

"My word, you are quick. Why yes, that would be me. But you aren't looking for me, are you? You're lookin' for ol' Redcap."

"Yes. Robin Redcap, if my information is correct."

"Aye, he thought you might be, and that you might be tryin' to spoil his fun before we go." Her eyes glittered. She brought up her hands and Mack saw that they were like claws with long, jagged fingernails. They glowed green and a dark energy crackled between the digits. "I think this world has had enough of you, Mr. Macklemore."

Macklemore nodded. "Sorry to disappoint you, but I know more than your name, and I thought I might run into you."

He held up his laptop.

She cackled. "That is your magic weapon? A portable computer?"

"You'd be surprised what you can pack into one these," Mack said.

Natosha woke from her lethargy. She tasted the copper of blood in her mouth. And it tasted like fury.

She looked up and she saw Skylar, who was her friend, and who she had a hard crush on…

Skylar being lifted up by a rope and start thrashing.

She could not move.

"Oh, dear sweet Jesus," she prayed. "I am so sorry."

When Bill Edmonds was a teenager, he'd gone hunting with his old man. Fred Edmonds had been a big man. He'd liked shotguns. He was a retired police officer, and he liked to shoot. He didn't much care what he shot when he hunted, but what he killed he brought home and cooked. Squirrels, ducks, quail. If he was damn lucky maybe a deer.

That was his rule, though. When Fred Edmonds shot something, he carried it home and he ate it. The family shared it, and though Fred was no gourmet, it was mostly good.

Bill had been eager to tag along on those hunting trips. This was time he could spend alone with his dad, no one else around to muddy things up. And when they were out, and Fred thought it was safe, he'd give his son Bill a buckshot gun.

It had taken a year or so of peeling tree bark with buckshot, but finally one beautiful fall Saturday, Bill had gotten himself a brace of quail.

Big Fred hooted and hollered all the way back home. "Son! Son! Quail! Good eating! I'm so damned proud of you."

Big Fred had showed Jim how to clean the quail. They'd baked them and eaten them. There was a bit of buckshot in Bill's bird, but Big Fred had warned him about that.

It was the most delicious meal that Bill had ever eaten.

Now, decades on, Bill didn't hadn't had a son. He would have liked to have had one. He'd met up with Maddy Harper and he thought she was a fine woman. And her son… well… This wasn't the kind of kid who went out blowing off buckshot in the woods to find his meaning in life. He was a good kid, though, and he had ways of his own.

Now Bill watched as this horror beyond horrors hauled Sky up toward the rafters, and there was nothing he could do. He still held the gun, but he couldn't lift it. He couldn't fire and even if he did, it probably wouldn't have much effect.

He wondered, if his dad had gotten a crack at this… goblin… if he'd have tried to barbecue it.

Isabella prayed softly under her breath, and she watched. She'd been caught by surprise, and cursed herself inwardly for not expecting something like this. Redcap was old and powerful. He spoke like a fool, but it was just his way. A deception to distract, like the various ways he chose to appear, depending on the situation. Like the ridiculous nooses when he could as easily have slipped into one home after another and had his way with whomever… unless it was the suicide.

She ran over the facts as she waited, relaxed, but taut. If the thing grew distracted or overconfident, she would act, and it would be swift. She had seen many creatures like this into their final graves.

Robin Redcap was beside himself with glee.

All of the waiting had been worth it. The old woman was out, keeping others away until it was complete, and he'd already fed—the fools in the house of books. They had been sweet—salted with hate and layered in resentment. It was the stuff that had kept him alive for so long, the source of his power.

They had been tasty, and they'd been more than he'd hoped for, but now there was so much more. When Skylar Harper had first appeared to him, he'd sensed something new—something immense. A deep, deep well of power to feast upon.

He had already grown immensely powerful. He felt it bulging in in his arms, stronger than it had felt in centuries. It dripped, sweet and red, from the brim of his cap.

Then he heard a huge crash, a sound that should not have been, and it shook him from his reverie. His concentration slipped, and he turned, startled.

The witch's cackle was like Satan's chalk on Hell's chalkboard.

"A laptop? Well then, *en garde*."

She came for him, fingernails growing into gleaming knives.

Mack wasted no time. He stepped nimbly aside, snapped the laptop closed, and in one smooth motion brought it around to crash into the back of the hag's skull. She screamed, and he jumped back. For once, he was glad he'd listened to Isabella. He was going to miss the laptop, but...

"What?" the crone screeched. "What have you..."

She staggered forward a step, reached out, as if she could grab something from the air, something he couldn't see. Mack pulled the laptop back and swung it again, driving her to her knees.

He spun, and this time he drove the metal corner of the laptop into her eye socket, flexing his muscled arms for more torque. His only distraction from the networks and data, the computers and the searches, was his search for the moments of pure adrenalin that only extreme sports could bring. He was an avid runner, skier, surfed when he could, and climbed rocks on weekends. He had the body of a jock wrapped around possibly the most complex geek-strong brain in existence, and he put every bit of that strength into that final shot.

"Technology began with physical breakthroughs," he said. "Like metallurgy. It's amazing how light this machine is, considering it's coated in pure, blessed silver."

There was no answer. The creature fell forward to her hands and knees. He brought the laptop down a final time, crushing what remained of the goblin queen's skull. She shriveled then, shrinking into herself, or seeping into the ground. Her clothing, her fancy coat, flattened and emptied as if she'd never existed.

Mack stared at the ground at his feet. Then he looked at the laptop. It was covered in gore, but that too burned and sizzled... and disappeared. The machine was ruined, crumpled and cracked... but he did not throw it aside. Its brain was dead, but the silver was still intact.

The huge plate glass window of the house that fronted the river exploded inward, shattering and spraying the room with a waterfall-like glitter of dust and glass. The shattered splinters sailed out into the room, ripping into everything.

They showered the giggling goblin, who had been hidden in

the shadows, making him glisten.

"I see him!" cried Isabella. "I see him!"

More to the point, though, was what was crashing through the window.

It came like some black bolt of lightning, something out of a ninja movie. Something unbelievably violent and filled with a fury beyond expression.

It landed in that shattered glass but was up in a quick roll, brandishing a large sharp sword. Without a moment's hesitation the figure swung the sword in a brilliant, flickering arc. As it sliced cleanly through the air, it struck the rope suspending Sky from the rafters and parted it as if it had never existed. The pressure on his throat released, Sky dropped to the floor with a thump.

"Samurai…ghostbuster!" cried Adam Even.

Face cut from glass but eyes wide and wild he turned to face the goblin, which was once more all but invisible. Having no clear target, he chose the attack that made the most sense. He swung the blade in a crisscross pattern, slicing empty air. Then he felt resistance, and where the blade struck, sparks flew and some sort of energy spurted into the air, like electricity suddenly freed from wires and shot into space.

In that moment, they were all free of the strange paralysis that had held them. Isabella Ferrara was the first to act. She cried out in Latin, even as she reached for one of the bottles of holy water and splashed out part of its contents in the direction of the spot where Adam Even's blade had struck. The liquid hissed and splattered. In one corner of the swirl, a figure flashed, gnarled but no longer a dwarf.

A red hat, redder than rage, shone in the darkness. What little light there was glimmered on that dripping, red nightmare. It was hideous, but it was *there*!

Adam Even instantly flung himself toward the monster bringing down the sword as hard as he could. He struck out and made contact with a shoulder. There was a scream and the ghost-lights around the thing flickered like red lightning.

Adam staggered and fell down.

"You!" Redcap snarled. "You!" The goblin took a step toward the fallen man.

"No way, you son of a bitch." Bill Edmunds's gun was in his hand and he pulled the trigger, again and again, bullets slamming into the thing and stopping its progress.

"More holy water!" Maddy cried.

One of the bottles that Isabella had lugged in was closest to Natosha. She was already unscrewing the top and fearlessly ran forward to the sparking creature. It didn't see her coming, and she splashed the bottle's contents full onto its form. Redcap lit up with angry flames that danced over his skin. He keened, coming fully visible. He was a thing of warped muscle and oozing pustules, with a nose like a gourd. His eyes burned like fiery lumps of coal.

It turned to flee.

Maddy scurried over to Sky. He was unconscious but still breathing. She pulled the noose from around his neck and checked to see if she needed to perform CPR. He was okay. He was okay!

Adam Even struggled to get up, but he fell again. "Damn you, damn you," he said.

"You bastard!" screeched Maddy. Without hesitation she grabbed the sharp samurai sword. With all her power and agility, she leaped at the goblin and swiped the blade full across his neck.

The sword sliced through its scaly hide and dug deep.

Robin Redcap gurgled. He staggered, his head tilting at an unnatural angle. He swiped back at Maddy and his solid arm knocked her off her feet and into the table, where she hit her head. The goblin, a contorted flurry of flailing limbs, made for the door, even though its head was almost lopped off.

It was rewarded for its efforts by more holy water, more Latin, and more gunshots.

But Adam Even was up again. He fumbled for the samurai sword, that bright gift from a long-lost friend.

"The head," cried Isabella. "Get the head!"

Staggering, Adam reached his feet. Somehow he achieved balance and ran forward. The edge of the blade whirled and found the other side of Redcap's neck. A flood of greenish slime and unspeakable gunk and the head fell back, attached to the shoulders only by some sort of spinal cord.

The goblin's burning eyes still glared back at his attackers, and he snarled and laughed raucously. As his body slumped to the floor, the spinal column, thick as a black snake, slipped out of the body like some weird, slimy serpent. It coiled and slithered and pushed the head toward the door.

"Damn," said Isabella. She ran forward, dumped more holy water over the thing.

Bill Edmonds stepped forward. "Keep that up. It'll go invisible otherwise." He lifted one booted foot and planted it on the writhing snake. Then the other, putting his full two hundred and twenty-two pounds on the thing.

Bill reached down, grabbed the head firmly on each side, managed to avoid the snapping teeth.

"I'll get you! I'll get you all. You'll see! You'll see!"

"Natosha. The kitchen light! The kitchen sink."

Natosha immediately obeyed. The lights flashed on in the kitchen. The snakelike spine writhed as Edmonds carried the head. "Fellow, you gotta help me out with that cutlery of yours."

"Would you believe I used to work at a Benihana?" said Adam Even.

It was a struggle, mostly because the writhing spine wanted to grab onto something, anything, but finally Edmonds got it into the kitchen and over the sink.

"Natosha," he said, "turn on the garbage disposal."

He slammed the goblin's leering, snapping head into the sink. Isabella dumped more holy water on it, and Adam Even stepped forward.

The powerful garbage disposal fired up.

"Gotcha," said Adam Even.

He stabbed the end of the snake tail and pushed it, pushed it hard as he could. It was just thin enough to push into the rubber opening and down into the snarling blades.

They started grinding.

It caught, and it started pulling.

Caught, unable to move, the goblin called Robin Redcap glared up at them, still defiant. With his left hand, Bill pushed down on the top of the slimy red cap. With the other he pulled his gun out and fired point blank into one of the thing's eyes. Then the other. Noxious green slime spurted into the sink.

"More water," he said.

Isabella tilted the jug she'd been holding, pouring it in a slow, steady stream over what remained of the thing's head. The snaky spine had been pulled all the way in by the garbage disposal but the head was stuck like a bloated plug. The teeth still gnashed and guttural curses in some ancient language filled the air.

"Don't crush that dwarf," said Adam Even. "Hand me the pliers."

He stepped forward and started stabbing downward with the Belushi sword. Stabbing and slicing, stabbing and slicing, doing his best to inflict the maximum damage in the confined space of the sink. He reduced it to a pulped, slivered mess, and the disposal began to gain ground. It took what seemed forever, but eventually the head was gone and the whole bottom of the stainless steel sink was filled with holy water, bubbling up sulphurous stink like something in a swamp.

Isabella crossed herself and threw in some sacramental wafers for good measure, allowing them to coil down into the sewer with the creature's ground-up remains.

"He was a good goblin," said Adam Even. "But he was a baaaaad boy."

And then he passed out, falling to the floor, splattering the bright linoleum with bright blood.

Epilogue

A few of the surviving human participants in what Wendell "Mack" Macklemore would later file under the name "The Noose Club" sat around in Geoffrey Bullfinch's large hospital room. Most of them were also staying at the hospital, but it was a visiting hour, so it was a good time to congregate.

There had been a long silence. The sun was going down in the west, and it looked as though the sky was exploding in elegant crimson and purple against the Cascades. A window was open and a bit of a wind whipped through, fanning out a white curtain into an almost-wraith.

"Sky, could you close that window?" said Madrigal Harper. "We'll all catch our death of cold."

No one laughed.

Skylar Harper got up and stiffly closed the window, constrained by his neck brace.

"That would be a lousy way to go," said Bullfinch, "after all that has happened. Pneumonia."

"I think I'd take that over some other options I never considered before this week." Bill Edmonds shivered and it had nothing to do with any cold that Maddy had felt. "Jesus. They're still trying to clean up the mess down at headquarters. Mad serial killers is what we're going to have to call it."

"I had a friend once who went fishing for the first time and caught pneumonia," said Adam Even, laughing weakly at his own joke.

"Actually," said Phil Roman, slumped in his wheel chair, "Pneumonia is an incredibly common way to die. And want to get it? Check in at a hospital." There was a pair of tubes coming out of his nose and going back to a small portable oxygen tank. Much of his skin was burned, but by some miracle, the Eugene Fire Department had managed to pull him out alive.

"The usual good cheer from Mr. Warmth," said Adam Even.

"Fuck you! You're not the one who lost a house full of incredibly valuable books!" grumbled the big fellow.

One whole side of his head was swathed in bandages and gauze. Blackened eyes peered through owlish glasses.

"What wasn't burned was soaked in blood." He shook his head. "Give me some of that quick-acting pneumonia. Please."

"Oh, come on, Mr. Roman," said Sky. "You're alive. Everyone was shocked you made it out of that house."

"Oh, it was my own fault," he said. "It was that damned Ralphie. Geez. Hard to admit this, but I was a fool. And now I've got nothing."

"You've got savings, right?"

"Less that you'd think. I had everything tied up in… my stuff."

"No insurance?" said Maddy.

Phil glared darkly.

"Your pension. Social Security?" said Maddy.

"Oh, sure."

"Oh, but Philip, my friend. You have your mind. Your vast knowledge. Just imagine all the fun you had over the years. Now you can start over…. And we can work on my part of it. I have many, many old volumes in my collection, and at Mack's insistence, I've had them digitized. I'm more than willing to sell them to you for a pittance."

Phil said nothing. He just sucked in oxygen.

But then a small smile crept on his lips.

"Okay, I'll stop with the sad-sack routine—for now. One thing, though. When we get out of here, and have dinner? No freaking pizza…"

The next evening after he was sure he'd collected every bit of useful data available, Mack left on a plane. He had a conference he had to attend in New York so he took a puddle jumper toward Seattle where he'd catch a red eye.

Things had been a little misty in Eugene, and now, as he slumped back sitting in the exit seat, he watched as the plane sailed up through the gray thatch of cloud cover, humming and grumbling and generally doing the plane-like things propeller planes did.

As the plane broke through the cloud cover, he caught a flash of movement through the window, a shadow sitting on the propeller hump. Doing something.

What? What the hell?

He blinked and the thing was gone.

An optical illusion. Surely...

But then he thought he saw the figure again, dancing on metal boots, a cap sailing bloody crimson in the flashing wind.

And then it was gone.

I've been watching too many Twilight Zone *episodes.*

When drinks came alone, he ordered a double Scotch. Then, grabbing the waitress by the arm, he winked.

"Better make it a triple."

The Goblin Market

By Christina Rosetti

Morning and evening
Maids heard the goblins cry:
"Come buy our orchard fruits,
Come buy, come buy:
Apples and quinces,
Lemons and oranges,
Plump unpeck'd cherries,
Melons and raspberries,
Bloom-down-cheek'd peaches,
Swart-headed mulberries,
Wild free-born cranberries,
Crab-apples, dewberries,
Pine-apples, blackberries,
Apricots, strawberries;—
All ripe together
In summer weather,—
Morns that pass by,
Fair eves that fly;
Come buy, come buy:
Our grapes fresh from the vine,
Pomegranates full and fine,
Dates and sharp bullaces,
Rare pears and greengages,
Damsons and bilberries,
Taste them and try:
Currants and gooseberries,
Bright-fire-like barberries,
Figs to fill your mouth,

Citrons from the South,
Sweet to tongue and sound to eye;
Come buy, come buy."
Evening by evening
Among the brookside rushes,
Laura bow'd her head to hear,
Lizzie veil'd her blushes:
Crouching close together
In the cooling weather,
With clasping arms and cautioning lips,
With tingling cheeks and finger tips.
"Lie close," Laura said,
Pricking up her golden head:
"We must not look at goblin men,
We must not buy their fruits:
Who knows upon what soil they fed
Their hungry thirsty roots?"
"Come buy," call the goblins
Hobbling down the glen.
"Oh," cried Lizzie, "Laura, Laura,
You should not peep at goblin men."
Lizzie cover'd up her eyes,
Cover'd close lest they should look;
Laura rear'd her glossy head,
And whisper'd like the restless brook:
"Look, Lizzie, look, Lizzie,
Down the glen tramp little men.
One hauls a basket,
One bears a plate,
One lugs a golden dish
Of many pounds weight.
How fair the vine must grow
Whose grapes are so luscious;
How warm the wind must blow
Through those fruit bushes."

"No," said Lizzie, "No, no, no;
Their offers should not charm us,
Their evil gifts would harm us."
She thrust a dimpled finger
In each ear, shut eyes and ran:
Curious Laura chose to linger
Wondering at each merchant man.
One had a cat's face,
One whisk'd a tail,
One tramp'd at a rat's pace,
One crawl'd like a snail,
One like a wombat prowl'd obtuse and furry,
One like a ratel tumbled hurry skurry.
She heard a voice like voice of doves
Cooing all together:
They sounded kind and full of loves
In the pleasant weather.
Laura stretch'd her gleaming neck
Like a rush-imbedded swan,
Like a lily from the beck,
Like a moonlit poplar branch,
Like a vessel at the launch
When its last restraint is gone.
Backwards up the mossy glen
Turn'd and troop'd the goblin men,
With their shrill repeated cry,
"Come buy, come buy."
When they reach'd where Laura was
They stood stock still upon the moss,
Leering at each other,
Brother with queer brother;
Signaling each other,
Brother with sly brother.
One set his basket down,
One rear'd his plate;

One began to weave a crown
Of tendrils, leaves, and rough nuts brown
(Men sell not such in any town);
One heav'd the golden weight
Of dish and fruit to offer her:
"Come buy, come buy," was still their cry.
Laura stared but did not stir,
Long'd but had no money:
The whisk-tail'd merchant bade her taste
In tones as smooth as honey,
The cat-faced purr'd,
The rat-faced spoke a word
Of welcome, and the snail-paced even was heard;
One parrot-voiced and jolly
Cried "Pretty Goblin" still for "Pretty Polly;"—
One whistled like a bird.
But sweet-tooth Laura spoke in haste:
"Good folk, I have no coin;
To take were to purloin:
I have no copper in my purse,
I have no silver either,
And all my gold is on the furze
That shakes in windy weather
Above the rusty heather."
"You have much gold upon your head,"
They answer'd all together:
"Buy from us with a golden curl."
She clipp'd a precious golden lock,
She dropp'd a tear more rare than pearl,
Then suck'd their fruit globes fair or red:
Sweeter than honey from the rock,
Stronger than man-rejoicing wine,
Clearer than water flow'd that juice;
She never tasted such before,
How should it cloy with length of use?

She suck'd and suck'd and suck'd the more
Fruits which that unknown orchard bore;
She suck'd until her lips were sore;
Then flung the emptied rinds away
But gather'd up one kernel stone,
And knew not was it night or day
As she turn'd home alone.
Lizzie met her at the gate
Full of wise upbraidings:
"Dear, you should not stay so late,
Twilight is not good for maidens;
Should not loiter in the glen
In the haunts of goblin men.
Do you not remember Jeanie,
How she met them in the moonlight,
Took their gifts both choice and many,
Ate their fruits and wore their flowers
Pluck'd from bowers
Where summer ripens at all hours?
But ever in the moonlight
She pined and pined away;
Sought them by night and day,
Found them no more, but dwindled and grew gray;
Then fell with the first snow,
While to this day no grass will grow
Where she lies low:
I planted daisies there a year ago
That never blow.
You should not loiter so."
"Nay, hush," said Laura:
"Nay, hush, my sister:
I ate and ate my fill,
Yet my mouth waters still;
To-morrow night I will
Buy more;" and kiss'd her:

"Have done with sorrow;
I'll bring you plums to-morrow
Fresh on their mother twigs,
Cherries worth getting;
You cannot think what figs
My teeth have met in,
What melons icy-cold
Piled on a dish of gold
Too huge for me to hold,
What peaches with a velvet nap,
Pellucid grapes without one seed:
Odorous indeed must be the mead
Whereon they grow, and pure the wave they drink
With lilies at the brink,
And sugar-sweet their sap."
Golden head by golden head, (the goblin read aloud)
Like two pigeons in one nest
Folded in each other's wings,
They lay down in their curtain'd bed:
Like two blossoms on one stem,
Like two flakes of new-fall'n snow,
Like two wands of ivory
Tipp'd with gold for awful kings.
Moon and stars gaz'd in at them,
Wind sang to them lullaby,
Lumbering owls forbore to fly,
Not a bat flapp'd to and fro
Round their rest:
Cheek to cheek and breast to breast
Lock'd together in one nest.
Early in the morning
When the first cock crow'd his warning,
Neat like bees, as sweet and busy,
Laura rose with Lizzie:
Fetch'd in honey, milk'd the cows,

Air'd and set to rights the house,
Kneaded cakes of whitest wheat,
Cakes for dainty mouths to eat,
Next churn'd butter, whipp'd up cream,
Fed their poultry, sat and sew'd;
Talk'd as modest maidens should:
Lizzie with an open heart,
Laura in an absent dream,
One content, one sick in part;
One warbling for the mere bright day's delight,
One longing for the night.
At length slow evening came:
They went with pitchers to the reedy brook;
Lizzie most placid in her look,
Laura most like a leaping flame.
They drew the gurgling water from its deep;
Lizzie pluck'd purple and rich golden flags,
Then turning homeward said: "The sunset flushes
Those furthest loftiest crags;
Come, Laura, not another maiden lags.
No wilful squirrel wags,
The beasts and birds are fast asleep."
But Laura loiter'd still among the rushes
And said the bank was steep.
And said the hour was early still
The dew not fall'n, the wind not chill;
Listening ever, but not catching
The customary cry,
"Come buy, come buy,"
With its iterated jingle
Of sugar-baited words:
Not for all her watching
Once discerning even one goblin
Racing, whisking, tumbling, hobbling;
Let alone the herds

That used to tramp along the glen,
In groups or single,
Of brisk fruit-merchant men.
Till Lizzie urged, "O Laura, come;
I hear the fruit-call but I dare not look:
You should not loiter longer at this brook:
Come with me home.
The stars rise, the moon bends her arc,
Each glowworm winks her spark,
Let us get home before the night grows dark:
For clouds may gather
Though this is summer weather,
Put out the lights and drench us through;
Then if we lost our way what should we do?"
Laura turn'd cold as stone
To find her sister heard that cry alone,
That goblin cry,
"Come buy our fruits, come buy."
Must she then buy no more such dainty fruit?
Must she no more such succous pasture find,
Gone deaf and blind?
Her tree of life droop'd from the root:
She said not one word in her heart's sore ache;
But peering thro' the dimness, nought discerning,
Trudg'd home, her pitcher dripping all the way;
So crept to bed, and lay
Silent till Lizzie slept;
Then sat up in a passionate yearning,
And gnash'd her teeth for baulk'd desire, and wept
As if her heart would break.
Day after day, night after night,
Laura kept watch in vain
In sullen silence of exceeding pain.
She never caught again the goblin cry:
"Come buy, come buy;"—

She never spied the goblin men
Hawking their fruits along the glen:
But when the noon wax'd bright
Her hair grew thin and gray;
She dwindled, as the fair full moon doth turn
To swift decay and burn
Her fire away.
One day remembering her kernel-stone
She set it by a wall that faced the south;
Dew'd it with tears, hoped for a root,
Watch'd for a waxing shoot,
But there came none;
It never saw the sun,
It never felt the trickling moisture run:
While with sunk eyes and faded mouth
She dream'd of melons, as a traveller sees
False waves in desert drouth
With shade of leaf-crown'd trees,
And burns the thirstier in the sandful breeze.
She no more swept the house,
Tended the fowls or cows,
Fetch'd honey, kneaded cakes of wheat,
Brought water from the brook:
But sat down listless in the chimney-nook
And would not eat.
Tender Lizzie could not bear
To watch her sister's cankerous care
Yet not to share.
She night and morning
Caught the goblins' cry:
"Come buy our orchard fruits,
Come buy, come buy;"—
Beside the brook, along the glen,
She heard the tramp of goblin men,
The yoke and stir

Poor Laura could not hear;
Long'd to buy fruit to comfort her,
But fear'd to pay too dear.
She thought of Jeanie in her grave,
Who should have been a bride;
But who for joys brides hope to have
Fell sick and died
In her gay prime,
In earliest winter time
With the first glazing rime,
With the first snow-fall of crisp winter time.
Till Laura dwindling
Seem'd knocking at Death's door:
Then Lizzie weigh'd no more
Better and worse;
But put a silver penny in her purse,
Kiss'd Laura, cross'd the heath with clumps of furze
At twilight, halted by the brook:
And for the first time in her life
Began to listen and look.
Laugh'd every goblin
When they spied her peeping:
Came towards her hobbling,
Flying, running, leaping,
Puffing and blowing,
Chuckling, clapping, crowing,
Clucking and gobbling,
Mopping and mowing,
Full of airs and graces,
Pulling wry faces,
Demure grimaces,
Cat-like and rat-like,
Ratel- and wombat-like,
Snail-paced in a hurry,
Parrot-voiced and whistler,

Helter skelter, hurry skurry,
Chattering like magpies,
Fluttering like pigeons,
Gliding like fishes,—
Hugg'd her and kiss'd her:
Squeez'd and caress'd her:
Stretch'd up their dishes,
Panniers, and plates:
"Look at our apples
Russet and dun,
Bob at our cherries,
Bite at our peaches,
Citrons and dates,
Grapes for the asking,
Pears red with basking
Out in the sun,
Plums on their twigs;
Pluck them and suck them,
Pomegranates, figs."—
"Good folk," said Lizzie,
Mindful of Jeanie:
"Give me much and many: —
Held out her apron,
Toss'd them her penny.
"Nay, take a seat with us,
Honour and eat with us,"
They answer'd grinning:
"Our feast is but beginning.
Night yet is early,
Warm and dew-pearly,
Wakeful and starry:
Such fruits as these
No man can carry:
Half their bloom would fly,
Half their dew would dry,

Half their flavour would pass by.
Sit down and feast with us,
Be welcome guest with us,
Cheer you and rest with us."—
"Thank you," said Lizzie: "But one waits
At home alone for me:
So without further parleying,
If you will not sell me any
Of your fruits though much and many,
Give me back my silver penny
I toss'd you for a fee."—
They began to scratch their pates,
No longer wagging, purring,
But visibly demurring,
Grunting and snarling.
One call'd her proud,
Cross-grain'd, uncivil;
Their tones wax'd loud,
Their looks were evil.
Lashing their tails
They trod and hustled her,
Elbow'd and jostled her,
Claw'd with their nails,
Barking, mewing, hissing, mocking,
Tore her gown and soil'd her stocking,
Twitch'd her hair out by the roots,
Stamp'd upon her tender feet,
Held her hands and squeez'd their fruits
Against her mouth to make her eat.
White and golden Lizzie stood,
Like a lily in a flood,—
Like a rock of blue-vein'd stone
Lash'd by tides obstreperously,—
Like a beacon left alone
In a hoary roaring sea,

Sending up a golden fire,—
Like a fruit-crown'd orange-tree
White with blossoms honey-sweet
Sore beset by wasp and bee,—
Like a royal virgin town
Topp'd with gilded dome and spire
Close beleaguer'd by a fleet
Mad to tug her standard down.
One may lead a horse to water,
Twenty cannot make him drink.
Though the goblins cuff'd and caught her,
Coax'd and fought her,
Bullied and besought her,
Scratch'd her, pinch'd her black as ink,
Kick'd and knock'd her,
Maul'd and mock'd her,
Lizzie utter'd not a word;
Would not open lip from lip
Lest they should cram a mouthful in:
But laugh'd in heart to feel the drip
Of juice that syrupp'd all her face,
And lodg'd in dimples of her chin,
And streak'd her neck which quaked like curd.
At last the evil people,
Worn out by her resistance,
Flung back her penny, kick'd their fruit
Along whichever road they took,
Not leaving root or stone or shoot;
Some writh'd into the ground,
Some div'd into the brook
With ring and ripple,
Some scudded on the gale without a sound,
Some vanish'd in the distance.
In a smart, ache, tingle,
Lizzie went her way;

Knew not was it night or day;
Sprang up the bank, tore thro' the furze,
Threaded copse and dingle,
And heard her penny jingle
Bouncing in her purse,—
Its bounce was music to her ear.
She ran and ran
As if she fear'd some goblin man
Dogg'd her with gibe or curse
Or something worse:
But not one goblin scurried after,
Nor was she prick'd by fear;
The kind heart made her windy-paced
That urged her home quite out of breath with haste
And inward laughter.
She cried, "Laura," up the garden,
"Did you miss me?
Come and kiss me.
Never mind my bruises,
Hug me, kiss me, suck my juices
Squeez'd from goblin fruits for you,
Goblin pulp and goblin dew.
Eat me, drink me, love me;
I have no copper in my purse,
I have no silver either,
And all my gold is on the furze
That shakes in windy weather
Above the rusty heather."
"You have much gold upon your head,"
They answer'd all together:
"Buy from us with a golden curl."
She clipp'd a precious golden lock,
She dropp'd a tear more rare than pearl,
Then suck'd their fruit globes fair or red:
Sweeter than honey from the rock,

Stronger than man-rejoicing wine,
Clearer than water flow'd that juice;
She never tasted such before,
How should it cloy with length of use?
She suck'd and suck'd and suck'd the more
Fruits which that unknown orchard bore;
She suck'd until her lips were sore;
Then flung the emptied rinds away
But gather'd up one kernel stone,
And knew not was it night or day
As she turn'd home alone.
Lizzie met her at the gate
Full of wise upbraidings:
"Dear, you should not stay so late,
Twilight is not good for maidens;
Should not loiter in the glen
In the haunts of goblin men.
Do you not remember Jeanie,
How she met them in the moonlight,
Took their gifts both choice and many,
Ate their fruits and wore their flowers
Pluck'd from bowers
Where summer ripens at all hours?
But ever in the noonlight
She pined and pined away;
Sought them by night and day,
Found them no more, but dwindled and grew gray;
Then fell with the first snow,
While to this day no grass will grow
Where she lies low:
I planted daisies there a year ago
That never blow.
You should not loiter so."
"Nay, hush," said Laura:
"Nay, hush, my sister:

I ate and ate my fill,
Yet my mouth waters still;
To-morrow night I will
Buy more;" and kiss'd her:
"Have done with sorrow;
I'll bring you plums to-morrow
Fresh on their mother twigs,
Cherries worth getting;
You cannot think what figs
My teeth have met in,
What melons icy-cold
Piled on a dish of gold
Too huge for me to hold,
What peaches with a velvet nap,
Pellucid grapes without one seed:
Odorous indeed must be the mead
Whereon they grow, and pure the wave they drink
With lilies at the brink,
And sugar-sweet their sap."
Golden head by golden head, (the goblin read aloud)
Like two pigeons in one nest
Folded in each other's wings,
They lay down in their curtain'd bed:
Like two blossoms on one stem,
Like two flakes of new-fall'n snow,
Like two wands of ivory
Tipp'd with gold for awful kings.
Moon and stars gaz'd in at them,
Wind sang to them lullaby,
Lumbering owls forbore to fly,
Not a bat flapp'd to and fro
Round their rest:
Cheek to cheek and breast to breast
Lock'd together in one nest.
Early in the morning

When the first cock crow'd his warning,
Neat like bees, as sweet and busy,
Laura rose with Lizzie:
Fetch'd in honey, milk'd the cows,
Air'd and set to rights the house,
Kneaded cakes of whitest wheat,
Cakes for dainty mouths to eat,
Next churn'd butter, whipp'd up cream,
Fed their poultry, sat and sew'd;
Talk'd as modest maidens should:
Lizzie with an open heart,
Laura in an absent dream,
One content, one sick in part;
One warbling for the mere bright day's delight,
One longing for the night.
At length slow evening came:
They went with pitchers to the reedy brook;
Lizzie most placid in her look,
Laura most like a leaping flame.
They drew the gurgling water from its deep;
Lizzie pluck'd purple and rich golden flags,
Then turning homeward said: "The sunset flushes
Those furthest loftiest crags;
Come, Laura, not another maiden lags.
No wilful squirrel wags,
The beasts and birds are fast asleep."
But Laura loiter'd still among the rushes
And said the bank was steep.
And said the hour was early still
The dew not fall'n, the wind not chill;
Listening ever, but not catching
The customary cry,
"Come buy, come buy,"
With its iterated jingle
Of sugar-baited words:

Not for all her watching
Once discerning even one goblin
Racing, whisking, tumbling, hobbling;
Let alone the herds
That used to tramp along the glen,
In groups or single,
Of brisk fruit-merchant men.
Till Lizzie urged, "O Laura, come;
I hear the fruit-call but I dare not look:
You should not loiter longer at this brook:
Come with me home.
The stars rise, the moon bends her arc,
Each glowworm winks her spark,
Let us get home before the night grows dark:
For clouds may gather
Though this is summer weather,
Put out the lights and drench us through;
Then if we lost our way what should we do?"
Laura turn'd cold as stone
To find her sister heard that cry alone,
That goblin cry,
"Come buy our fruits, come buy."
Must she then buy no more such dainty fruit?
Must she no more such succous pasture find,
Gone deaf and blind?
Her tree of life droop'd from the root:
She said not one word in her heart's sore ache;
But peering thro' the dimness, nought discerning,
Trudg'd home, her pitcher dripping all the way;
So crept to bed, and lay
Silent till Lizzie slept;
Then sat up in a passionate yearning,
And gnash'd her teeth for baulk'd desire, and wept
As if her heart would break.
Day after day, night after night,

Laura kept watch in vain
In sullen silence of exceeding pain.
She never caught again the goblin cry:
"Come buy, come buy;"—
She never spied the goblin men
Hawking their fruits along the glen:
But when the noon wax'd bright
Her hair grew thin and gray;
She dwindled, as the fair full moon doth turn
To swift decay and burn
Her fire away.
One day remembering her kernel-stone
She set it by a wall that faced the south;
Dew'd it with tears, hoped for a root,
Watch'd for a waxing shoot,
But there came none;
It never saw the sun,
It never felt the trickling moisture run:
While with sunk eyes and faded mouth
She dream'd of melons, as a traveller sees
False waves in desert drouth
With shade of leaf-crown'd trees,
And burns the thirstier in the sandful breeze.
She no more swept the house,
Tended the fowls or cows,
Fetch'd honey, kneaded cakes of wheat,
Brought water from the brook:
But sat down listless in the chimney-nook
And would not eat.
Tender Lizzie could not bear
To watch her sister's cankerous care
Yet not to share.
She night and morning
Caught the goblins' cry:
"Come buy our orchard fruits,

Come buy, come buy;"—
Beside the brook, along the glen,
She heard the tramp of goblin men,
The yoke and stir
Poor Laura could not hear;
Long'd to buy fruit to comfort her,
But fear'd to pay too dear.
She thought of Jeanie in her grave,
Who should have been a bride;
But who for joys brides hope to have
Fell sick and died
In her gay prime,
In earliest winter time
With the first glazing rime,
With the first snow-fall of crisp winter time.
Till Laura dwindling
Seem'd knocking at Death's door:
Then Lizzie weigh'd no more
Better and worse;
But put a silver penny in her purse,
Kiss'd Laura, cross'd the heath with clumps of furze
At twilight, halted by the brook:
And for the first time in her life
Began to listen and look.
Laugh'd every goblin
When they spied her peeping:
Came towards her hobbling,
Flying, running, leaping,
Puffing and blowing,
Chuckling, clapping, crowing,
Clucking and gobbling,
Mopping and mowing,
Full of airs and graces,
Pulling wry faces,
Demure grimaces,

Cat-like and rat-like,
Ratel- and wombat-like,
Snail-paced in a hurry,
Parrot-voiced and whistler,
Helter skelter, hurry skurry,
Chattering like magpies,
Fluttering like pigeons,
Gliding like fishes,—
Hugg'd her and kiss'd her:
Squeez'd and caress'd her:
Stretch'd up their dishes,
Panniers, and plates:
"Look at our apples
Russet and dun,
Bob at our cherries,
Bite at our peaches,
Citrons and dates,
Grapes for the asking,
Pears red with basking
Out in the sun,
Plums on their twigs;
Pluck them and suck them,
Pomegranates, figs."—
"Good folk," said Lizzie,
Mindful of Jeanie:
"Give me much and many: —
Held out her apron,
Toss'd them her penny.
"Nay, take a seat with us,
Honour and eat with us,"
They answer'd grinning:
"Our feast is but beginning.
Night yet is early,
Warm and dew-pearly,
Wakeful and starry:

Such fruits as these
No man can carry:
Half their bloom would fly,
Half their dew would dry,
Half their flavour would pass by.
Sit down and feast with us,
Be welcome guest with us,
Cheer you and rest with us."—
"Thank you," said Lizzie: "But one waits
At home alone for me:
So without further parleying,
If you will not sell me any
Of your fruits though much and many,
Give me back my silver penny
I toss'd you for a fee."—
They began to scratch their pates,
No longer wagging, purring,
But visibly demurring,
Grunting and snarling.
One call'd her proud,
Cross-grain'd, uncivil;
Their tones wax'd loud,
Their looks were evil.
Lashing their tails
They trod and hustled her,
Elbow'd and jostled her,
Claw'd with their nails,
Barking, mewing, hissing, mocking,
Tore her gown and soil'd her stocking,
Twitch'd her hair out by the roots,
Stamp'd upon her tender feet,
Held her hands and squeez'd their fruits
Against her mouth to make her eat.
White and golden Lizzie stood,
Like a lily in a flood,—

Like a rock of blue-vein'd stone
Lash'd by tides obstreperously,—
Like a beacon left alone
In a hoary roaring sea,
Sending up a golden fire,—
Like a fruit-crown'd orange-tree
White with blossoms honey-sweet
Sore beset by wasp and bee,—
Like a royal virgin town
Topp'd with gilded dome and spire
Close beleaguer'd by a fleet
Mad to tug her standard down.
One may lead a horse to water,
Twenty cannot make him drink.
Though the goblins cuff'd and caught her,
Coax'd and fought her,
Bullied and besought her,
Scratch'd her, pinch'd her black as ink,
Kick'd and knock'd her,
Maul'd and mock'd her,
Lizzie utter'd not a word;
Would not open lip from lip
Lest they should cram a mouthful in:
But laugh'd in heart to feel the drip
Of juice that syrupp'd all her face,
And lodg'd in dimples of her chin,
And streak'd her neck which quaked like curd.
At last the evil people,
Worn out by her resistance,
Flung back her penny, kick'd their fruit
Along whichever road they took,
Not leaving root or stone or shoot;
Some writh'd into the ground,
Some div'd into the brook
With ring and ripple,

Some scudded on the gale without a sound,
Some vanish'd in the distance.
In a smart, ache, tingle,
Lizzie went her way;
Knew not was it night or day;
Sprang up the bank, tore thro' the furze,
Threaded copse and dingle,
And heard her penny jingle
Bouncing in her purse,—
Its bounce was music to her ear.
She ran and ran
As if she fear'd some goblin man
Dogg'd her with gibe or curse
Or something worse:
But not one goblin scurried after,
Nor was she prick'd by fear;
The kind heart made her windy-paced
That urged her home quite out of breath with haste
And inward laughter.
She cried, "Laura," up the garden,
"Did you miss me?
Come and kiss me.
Never mind my bruises,
Hug me, kiss me, suck my juices
Squeez'd from goblin fruits for you,
Goblin pulp and goblin dew.
Eat me, drink me, love me;
Laura, make much of me;
For your sake I have braved the glen
And had to do with goblin merchant men."
Laura started from her chair,
Flung her arms up in the air,
Clutch'd her hair:
"Lizzie, Lizzie, have you tasted
For my sake the fruit forbidden?

Must your light like mine be hidden,
Your young life like mine be wasted,
Undone in mine undoing,
And ruin'd in my ruin,
Thirsty, canker'd, goblin-ridden?"—
She clung about her sister,
Kiss'd and kiss'd and kiss'd her:
Tears once again
Refresh'd her shrunken eyes,
Dropping like rain
After long sultry drouth;
Shaking with aguish fear, and pain,
She kiss'd and kiss'd her with a hungry mouth.
Her lips began to scorch,
That juice was wormwood to her tongue,
She loath'd the feast:
Writhing as one possess'd she leap'd and sung,
Rent all her robe, and wrung
Her hands in lamentable haste,
And beat her breast.
Her locks stream'd like the torch
Borne by a racer at full speed,
Or like the mane of horses in their flight,
Or like an eagle when she stems the light
Straight toward the sun,
Or like a caged thing freed,
Or like a flying flag when armies run.
Swift fire spread through her veins, knock'd at her heart,
Met the fire smouldering there
And overbore its lesser flame;
She gorged on bitterness without a name:
Ah! fool, to choose such part
Of soul-consuming care!
Sense fail'd in the mortal strife:
Like the watch-tower of a town

Which an earthquake shatters down,
Like a lightning-stricken mast,
Like a wind-uprooted tree
Spun about,
Like a foam-topp'd waterspout
Cast down headlong in the sea,
She fell at last;
Pleasure past and anguish past,
Is it death or is it life?
Life out of death.
That night long Lizzie watch'd by her,
Counted her pulse's flagging stir,
Felt for her breath,
Held water to her lips, and cool'd her face
With tears and fanning leaves:
But when the first birds chirp'd about their eaves,
And early reapers plodded to the place
Of golden sheaves,
And dew-wet grass
Bow'd in the morning winds so brisk to pass,
And new buds with new day
Open'd of cup-like lilies on the stream,
Laura awoke as from a dream,
Laugh'd in the innocent old way,
Hugg'd Lizzie but not twice or thrice;
Her gleaming locks show'd not one thread of gray,
Her breath was sweet as May
And light danced in her eyes.
Days, weeks, months, years
Afterwards, when both were wives
With children of their own;
Their mother-hearts beset with fears,
Their lives bound up in tender lives;
Laura would call the little ones
And tell them of her early prime,

Those pleasant days long gone
Of not-returning time:
Would talk about the haunted glen,
The wicked, quaint fruit-merchant men,
Their fruits like honey to the throat
But poison in the blood;
(Men sell not such in any town):
Would tell them how her sister stood
In deadly peril to do her good,
And win the fiery antidote:
Then joining hands to little hands
Would bid them cling together,
"For there is no friend like a sister
In calm or stormy weather;
To cheer one on the tedious way,
To fetch one if one goes astray,
To lift one if one totters down,
To strengthen whilst one stands."

Alison Gross

(traditional)

Alison Gross that lives in yon tower
The ugliest witch in the North Country
Has trysted me one day up to her bower
And many a fair speech she made to me
She stroked my head and she combed my hair
She set me down softly on her knee
Saying if you will be my lover so true
So many good things I would h
Go far away and let me be
I never will be your lover so true
And wish I were out of your communy

Chorus:
Alison Gross she must be
The ugliest witch in the North Country
Alison Gross she must be
The ugliest witch in the North Country

She showed me a mantle of red scarlet
With golden flowers and fringes fine
Saying if you will be my lover so true
This goodly gift it shall be thine
She showed me a shirt of the softest silk
Well wrought with pearls abound the band
Saying if you will be my lover so true
This goodly gift you shall command

Chorus

She showed me a cup of the good red gold
Well set with jewels so fair to see
Saying if you will be my lover so true
This goodly gift I will give to thee
Away, away, you ugly witch
Go far away and let me be
I never would kiss your ugly mouth
For all of the gifts that you could give

Chorus

She turned her right and round about
And thrice she blew on a grass-green horn
She swore by the moon and the stars of above
That she'd make me rue the day I was born
The out she has taken a silver wand
She's turned her three times round and round
She muttered such words till my strength it did fail
And she's turned me into an ugly worm

Chorus

About the Author

David **Bischoff** has published over 100 books, both fiction and non-fiction as well as over 100 short stories and who knows how many non-fiction articles. He has worked in various genres including horror, science fiction and fantasy, mystery and historical

His books include *Nightworld*, *The Selkie* and *The Judas Cross*. Bischoff has also worked in TV, starting with a stint at *NBC Washington* followed by freelance work for Disney, Marvel, DC, 4Kids and Paramount. He has credits for two *Star Trek: The Next Generation* scripts, "First Contact" and "Tin Woodman."

Although born in the Washington, D.C. area, he now lives in Eugene, Oregon.

Curious about other Crossroad Press books?
Stop by our site:
http://store.crossroadpress.com
We offer quality writing
in digital, audio, and print formats.

Enter the code FIRSTBOOK
to get 20% off your first order from our store!
Stop by today!